I0647749

The Enduring Faulkner

M.E. Bradford

The Enduring Faulkner:
Essays by M. E. Bradford, 1962-1992

Edited with an Introduction

by

Jack Trotter

Abbeville Institute Press

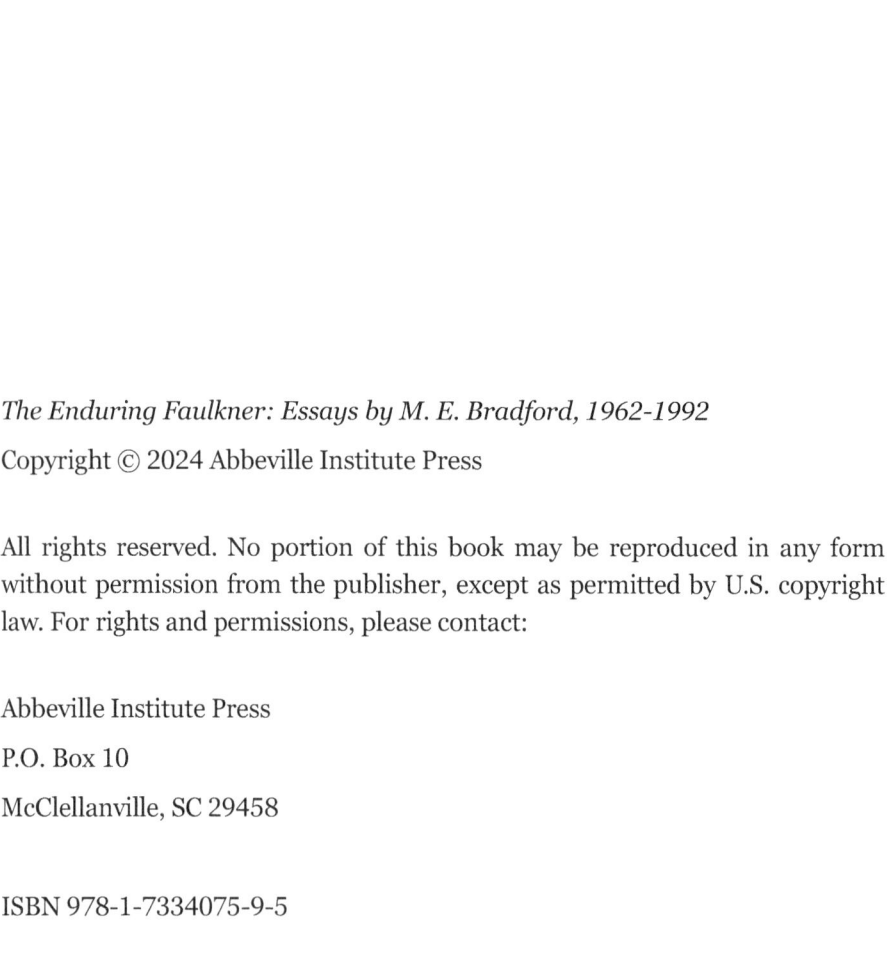

The Enduring Faulkner: Essays by M. E. Bradford, 1962-1992

Copyright © 2024 Abbeville Institute Press

All rights reserved. No portion of this book may be reproduced in any form without permission from the publisher, except as permitted by U.S. copyright law. For rights and permissions, please contact:

Abbeville Institute Press

P.O. Box 10

McClellanville, SC 29458

ISBN 978-1-7334075-9-5

First Edition

10 9 8 7 6 5 4 3 2 1

Contents

Introduction..vii

1. Faulkner's "Tall Men" 1

2. Faulkner and the Great White Father 15

3. Escaping Westward: Faulkner's "Golden Land" 23

4. Faulkner and the Jeffersonian Dream: Nationalism
   in "Two Soldiers" and "Shall Not Perish" 31

5. Faulkner's "Tomorrow" and the Plain People...................41

6. The Winding Horn: Hunting and the Making of
   Men in Faulkner's "Race at Morning"...............................49

7. "Spotted Horses" and the Short Cut to Paradise:
   A Note on the Endurance Theme in Faulkner.................59

8. The Gum Tree Scene: Observations on the
   Structure of "The Bear"[146] 67

9. All the Daughters of Eve:
   "Was" and the Unity of *Go Down, Moses* 77

10. On the Importance of Discovering God: Faulkner and
    Hemingway's "The Old Man and the Sea" 85

11. Family and Community in Faulkner's
    "Barn Burning" 91

12. Faulkner's "A Courtship":
    An Accommodation of Cultures 101

13. The Anomaly of Faulkner's World War I Stories 109

14. A Coda to Sartoris: Faulkner's "My Grandmother
    Millard and General Nathan Bedford Forrest
    and the Battle of Harrykin Creek".................................129

15. Text and Context:
    Reading Faulkner's *Intruder in the Dust*......................139

16. The Great Enterprise 149

Introduction

In an essay written over two decades ago, entitled "The Education of Mel Bradford: The Vanderbilt Years," Thomas Landess recalls his first meeting with Bradford in 1959, when both were graduate students: That meeting took place "on the stairway of Old Central, the building that for a time housed the Vanderbilt English Department.... I remember him standing on the stairway, bending down to shake my hand—tall and underfed, with enormous blue eyes. He'd come there from the University of Oklahoma, where he'd majored in philosophy and was something of a neo-Hegelian. By the time he he'd completed his doctoral work, there was none of that left." Over 30 years later, I, too, experienced the great pleasure of meeting Dr. Bradford at Vanderbilt during my own tenure there as an English graduate student. By then, he was still a striking figure, but no longer "underfed."

That was in the early 1990s. He was by then a distinguished professor at the University of Dallas but traveled to Vanderbilt periodically to lecture on literary matters, and particularly on the work of William Faulkner. While my memory of the details of those talks has faded, I remember vividly the sheer *presence* of the man, who loomed large both physically and intellectually. While I had in my early years read a good deal of Southern literature, including enough Faulkner to imagine that I knew something about the great novelist, I became aware, as I listened to Bradford's impassioned talks, that I was quite ignorant of Faulkner's real importance. As a Southerner, I was proud of Faulkner's national and international distinction, but had only begun to understand the Mississippian's role as a defender of Southern culture and tradition—a defense rooted in an imaginative reconstruction of the Southern *habitus* in the years after Mr. Lincoln's War and into the early twentieth century. The last time I saw Dr. Bradford was in the Spring of 1992— in retrospect an especially poignant occasion since he would be dead a year later. After another of his Faulkner talks, our host Dr. Harold Weatherby (known affectionately by some of his students as "Prince Hal") arranged that Dr. Bradford would join a few of us for a late lunch and a round or two of drinks at one of the watering holes just off campus, only a few blocks from Music Row. He was in fine spirits that day and regaled us with anecdotes about Faulkner, Donald Davidson, and country music.

Like his mentor Davidson, who had been a lifelong fan of Southern mountain balladry, he found much to admire in the country music tradition, especially in how it preserved a sense of family and place, but was less optimistic than Davidson had been that country music, having been relentlessly commercialized for many decades, could be depended upon to keep alive the flame of authenticity that the Carter family and other balladeers carried with them out of the hills when the first electrical country music recordings were cut in wax in Bristol, Tennessee in 1927.

Melvin Eustis Bradford, however, exuded authenticity from every pore. His work, spanning more than three decades, was wide ranging: from southern letters and culture to the Founding Fathers and the origins of the Constitution; to Abraham Lincoln and the "heresy" of equality; to conservative politics and much more. His writing most often took the form of essays. While he was trained in an academic setting, only a handful of his essays were, strictly speaking, aimed exclusively at academic audiences. His prose is always lucid and unencumbered with critical jargon. All told, he produced well over 300 essays and reviews, a number of which he assembled for later publication in his books—including *Generations of the Faithful Heart* (1983), *Remembering Who We Are: Observations of a*

Southern Conservative (1985), and *The Reactionary Imperative* (1991), just to mention the best known. Bradford's earliest essay on Faulkner was written in 1962. From the beginning he regarded the Mississippian as the foremost exemplar of what is sometimes called the Southern Renaissance. Forty-five of his essays and reviews were concerned with Faulkner's novels and short stories. Of those, he included only 9 in his books,[1] leaving a body of 36 essays on Faulkner that have remained, until now, uncollected. One of the aims of the present collection is to rescue the best of those uncollected essays from literary oblivion. The inspiration for this endeavor has been provided entirely by Dr. Clyde Wilson, who selected the essays. That is as it should be, for few living scholars are as well-versed in Bradford's life and work.[2]

The 16 essays included here range over a variety of Faulkner's literary productions, though the emphasis lies especially on the shorter fiction—both widely known and studied stories like "Barn Burning" and lesser-known texts like "Golden Land." Thematically, the essays reflect, of course, Bradford's own personal predilections, though there is no doubt that the recurring themes were also central to Faulkner's aims as a writer: the profound gravity of the past as it informs the present; the "peculiar" and tragic—even mythic—trajectory of Southern history; the powerful sense of place and attachment to the land; the importance not only of the old Southern hierarchies—especially the legacy of the antebellum planter class—

---

1 The essays on Faulkner previously included in Bradford's books are as follows: "Faulkner's *The Unvanquished*: The High Cost of Survival" and "What Grandfather Said: The Social Testimony of Faulkner's *The Reivers*" in *Generations of the Faithful Heart* (1983); "Faulkner's Last Words and the American Dilemma" in *Remembering Who We Are* (1985); "Artists at Home: Frost and Faulkner," "Brotherhood in *The Bear*" and "Brother, Son, and Heir: The Structural Focus of Faulkner's *Absalom, Absalom!*" in *The Reactionary Imperative* (1990); "A Studied Myopia: Faulkner and the New Literary History" and "Addie Bundren and the Design of *As I Lay Dying*" in *Against the Barbarians* (1992).

2 See *A Defense of Southern Conservatism: M.E. Bradford and His Achievements*, ed. Clyde N. Wilson (University of Missouri Press, 1999). In addition to a collection of essays about Bradford's work, this volume includes the definitive Bradford bibliography, assembled by Alan Cornett.

but also of the yeomanry or "plain folk"; and the preeminent moral 1importance of *endurance*. This list is hardly exhaustive, and I will elaborate on just a few of these themes in what follows:

First, however, I will offer some remarks on the idea of *romanitas*. The term refers not so much to a literary theme as to an overarching notion of Southern cultural and social coherence. Fortunately, Bradford himself commented at some length on this matter in "That Other Republic: *Romanitas* in Southern Literature,"[3] where he argues that the literatures of both ancient Rome and of the American South both reflect the "corporate spirit" of their respective cultures. This is not at all akin to the banal claim that works of literature reflect their historical context and circumstances. What Bradford means is that literary works in certain cultures, especially pre-modern cultures, speak with the collective voice of that culture, and take as given its moral priorities and social values. So powerful is the shared identity and cohesiveness of such cultures that the writers they produce naturally assume a public role. They do not seek to create mere artifacts that express their own subjective experience, as if their individual perception were somehow prior to that of the culture; nor do they set themselves apart from their culture, like Percy Shelley, who proclaimed grandiloquently that the great poets are the "unacknowledged legislators" of the world—as if the poet were necessarily a man without a home, a vagabond of the spirit who, because he has effectively renounced all provincial loyalties, has acquired the right to instruct the world at large.

From its beginnings in the seventeenth century, Southern culture was steeped in the literature of Rome—in Cicero, Horace, Virgil and the historians.[4] This was to some extent also true of the North in the colonial era, but with a difference. Northern educators and writers absorbed Roman texts through the lens of the Enlightenment, and

---

3   In the *Southern Humanities Review* Vol. 11 (1977), 4-13.

4   The influence of classical, and especially Roman, literature on Southern culture has recently been explored at some length by James Everett Kibler, Jr., in *The Classical Origins of Southern Literature* (Abbeville Institute, Ltd., Second Edition, June 2023). See also Kibler's *Faulkner the Southerner and the Continuity of Southern Letters* (McClellanville, SC: Abbeville Institute Press, 2023).

they tended to focus on republican principles outside the context of *romanitas*; whereas in the South, republican principles were fused with the Roman *habitus*—family, patriarchy, piety, military valor, and honor. One of the most powerful recurring images in Southern letters is that of Virgil's hero Aeneas saving his son and his father from the burning city of Troy before setting out for Italy, where he would become the father of the Roman people. As Bradford notes, the Virginian George Washington commissioned a bronze sculpture of this scene and displayed it on his mantle in the years after the Revolution. From the Southern perspective, there was a mythic continuity between the founding of Rome and the founding of America.

In Southern literature (understood broadly to encompass poetry, fiction, and non-fictional works), the Roman emphasis on the virtue inherent in agriculture and the rural life—as in Cato the Elder and, again, Virgil—is evident in celebrated colonial and antebellum works like John Taylor of Caroline's *Arator* or William Grayson's "The Hireling and the Slave," which Bradford identifies as a verse variant on the Horatian "moral essay." But the same attachment to the land is evident in early twentieth century works like Elizabeth Madox Roberts' *The Great Meadow*, Stark Young's *So Red the Rose*, and many novels, poems and essays produced by the Nashville Agrarians.

This tradition of republican virtue and veneration for the land and its people is evident throughout William Faulkner's mature work. Virtually everything that Faulkner wrote (with a few notable exceptions) is situated in rural Mississippi, and more particularly in the mythic Yoknapatawpha County, which might be regarded as a microcosm of the Deep South. Within that context Faulkner is always acutely aware of the long *durée* of historical struggle and conflict—of the travails of those who settled the land, of the Chickasaw Indians[5] whom the settlers displaced, of the complex mingling of black and white, of the tragic consequences of the War,

---

5   Two of the Bradford essays included in this volume are focused on Faulkner's Indian tales, or, more accurately, tales in which Indian characters play significant roles. Most of these tales are set in the period before the Indian Removal Act of 1830, or shortly

and of the rise of the New South—that is, the commercial, non-agrarian South—as represented by the Snopes clan. He is mindful, too, of the integrity and independence of the yeomanry—those men and women Bradford calls the "plain folk," following the example of Frank Owsley, whose study *The Plain Folk of the Old South* (1949) documented the lives and work of the white farmers who, as independent small landowners, perhaps more than any other segment of the Southern population had sustained and exemplified the ancient republican spirit.

Faulkner's understanding of the plain folk is drawn from his own personal acquaintance with them, but they are depicted very much in the way that Owsley describes them. Their forefathers were Scots clansmen or Scots-Irish who migrated to Mississippi by way of the Carolinas and the Tennessee mountains in the early nineteenth century, bringing with them their Calvinism and their patriarchal code of honor. They settled often in the hill country and cared little for wealth; what mattered was their land, their loyalty to kith and kin, and their prideful sense of independence. Among the most memorable of these families are the McCallums, who appear in several of Faulkner's novels and short stories, including *Sartoris*, *Intruder in the Dust*, and the fine short work "The Tall Men" (1941).

Bradford, in "Faulkner's 'Tall Men'" (Chap. 1), claims that the McCallums, more than any of the plain folk families in Faulkner's work, exemplify the virtues of their kind, especially their independence. When a district draft board agent comes calling at the McCallums' house, accompanied by a local marshal, to serve a warrant on Buddy McCallum's twin sons, who have failed to register, he is surprised to find that the McCallums are not at all what he assumed they would be. He expected to find a good-for-nothing, poor white family with no sense of their responsibility to their country. He finds Buddy laid up with a maimed leg, in great pain, and his gracious manner takes the agent off guard. When the McCallum patriarch learns of the agent's business, he explains that he had disregarded the notices

---

thereafter. See "Faulkner's 'A Courtship': An Accommodation of Cultures" (which deals with one of Faulkner's best comic stories), and "Faulkner and the Great White Father," which deals primarily with the tale entitled "Lo."

from the draft board because his experience with the government had taught him to be wary of signing government documents. Now, faced with a personal request, he doesn't hesitate to instruct his boys to go straight to the state capitol and register, which they do without protest. As Bradford explains, government papers had come to represent "man's surrender of responsibility for himself, his loss of personal importance, honor, and self-respect." But Buddy himself had served in World War I, just as his own father, Anse McCullum, had served the Confederacy. What Anse learned from that experience was "pride and humility: he had learned humility from defeat; and from defeat and his struggle during Reconstruction times, he learned to rebuild his life, had learned the necessity of pride ...."

These terms, pride and humility, which might at first seem antithetical, are the essential virtues of "endurance," a theme that one finds frequently in Faulkner's tales. Bradford, in the essays here, emphasizes the theme so often that we are left with the strong impression that endurance, as Faulkner understands it, is something like the cornerstone of the Southern moral edifice. Pride, in this context must be understood, not as the overweening pride of a man who lacks humility, but as the pride that arises out of the ownership of land, of being free of indebtedness—more generally, the pride of an independent man. As Bradford explains it in his wonderful analysis of "Faulkner's 'Tomorrow' and the Plain People" (Chap. 5), the pride of the yeomanry is all that they have, "but it is what they and their kin in Yoknapatawpha live on, and Faulkner admires them for it." Yet theirs is a pride which is "balanced by the humility implicit in their endurance of impossible circumstances," meaning circumstances over which they have no control. From such endurance arises "dignity."

The endurance theme is an important aspect of a number of the essays in this volume. Aside from the two already mentioned, the reader may also find eloquent discussions of the theme in "Escaping Westward, Faulkner's 'Golden Land'" (Chap. 3); "The Winding Horn: Hunting and the Making of Men in Faulkner's 'Race at Morning'" (Chap 6); "The Gum Tree Scene: Observations on the Structure of 'The Bear'" (Chap. 8); "All the Daughters of Eve:

'Was' and the Unity of *Go Down, Moses*" (Chap. 9); and "On the Importance of Discovering God: Faulkner and Hemingway's *The Old Man and the Sea*" (Chap. 10). Yet while all of these essays are splendid examples of Bradford's grasp of the Faulknerian moral vision, the most penetrating exposition of the idea of endurance can be found in "'Spotted Horses' and the Short Cut to Paradise: A Note on the Endurance Theme in Faulkner"[6] (Chap. 7). "Spotted Horses" signals the inaugural appearance of the unscrupulous Flem Snopes in Faulkner's fiction—the man who epitomizes everything that the Snopes' tribe represents—the materialist greed that recognizes no moral order. Appropriately, Flem first appears as a capitalist of sorts, who preys upon "one of the most fundamental human weaknesses," as Bradford notes, "the desire to get something for nothing, to find a short cut to bliss." In short, Flem and his sidekick, Buck Hipps, auction off a small herd of wild, spotted horses they have brought in from the southwest. Their chosen victims are the men of the hill country above Frenchman's Bend[7]—plain folk who should know better than to offer up hard earned dollars for untamed horses that have no practical use as farm animals. But Flem and Buck play upon their willingness to believe that they will get a bargain—and more than that, upon their masculine admiration for powerful horses.

But immediately upon the conclusion of the auction, the buyers become "aware of the problem of taking possession of their purchases." As Bradford memorably explains, the men are still in a "dazed and spellbound frame of mind ... [when] their foolishness comes down on them in the form of a stampede ... and a fruitless nocturnal chase." On the morning following, they must face the truth of their foolhardy pride—for pride, the wrong sort of pride, had led them to seek ownership of something beyond their natural capacity to control. Much of this wonderful story is, of course, comedy, but the underlying lesson is quite serious: The men who purchased these phantom horses had not yet been properly educated by experience

---

6   Faulkner's "Spotted Horses" was first published by *Scribner's Magazine* in June, 1931, then expanded and included in his novel *The Hamlet* (1940) as its first chapter.

7   Frenchman's Bend is the fictitious region of Yoknapatawpha where most of Faulkner's plain folk reside.

in endurance. Had they learned that lesson, they would not have been "subject to the machinations of a Flem Snopes because [such men] are not often governed by those particular impulses which would play them into hands of a Snopes."

I have mentioned the importance of the "corporate spirit" of the South, a spirit pervasive in Faulkner's Yoknapatawpha tales. The nature of that corporate spirit was often misunderstood (or not understood at all) by the Northern commentariat or its allies in liberal New York literary circles. An instance of this is the reception of *Intruder in the Dust* (1948), a novel that deals with the antagonisms generated by the "color line" at a time when the movement for desegregation was well underway. While Bradford had previously dealt with Faulkner's position on desegregation, he did not give extensive attention to *Intruder* until 1992 in "Text and Context: Reading Faulkner's *Intruder in the Dust*" (Chap. 15). Readers will find this selection especially illuminating, since it is perhaps the only literary critique of the novel which combines both a full understanding of the novel's thematic center and a sympathetic perception of the South's struggle, in the latter days of Jim Crow, to find a fair and equitable solution to the racial problem.

The plot is simple enough and is not without some of the elements of a murder mystery. When an elderly mulatto, Lucas Beauchamp, is accused of murdering a white man, Charles "Chick" Mallison,[8] the youngest of the Mallison offspring, seeks to find the evidence that will exonerate Lucas, a man whom Chick admires and regards as a friend. Chick's efforts to unearth the evidence he needs unfold against a backdrop of racial turmoil as many of the residents of Yoknapatawpha are all too eager to lynch Lucas, especially since several facts point to him, at least superficially, as the perpetrator of the crime. Chick is aided by his uncle, the lawyer Gavin Stevens, who in certain respects voices Faulkner's own views on the racial question in several extended speeches in the third part of the novel.

---

8   Readers of *The Town* (1957) will recognize Charles Mallison as one of the narrators of that novel. He also appears as the nephew of Gavin Stevens in a number of the tales included in *Knight's Gambit* (1949). The Mallison family is among the oldest and most prominent in Jefferson, the Yoknapatawpha county seat. [Ed.]

Bradford establishes convincingly that although most of the critical attention bestowed on the novel has focused on Beauchamp as the victim of vicious racial prejudice, the real center of the tale is Chick, who is a kind of knight errant in a story of chivalry. Though he is only 16 years old, he is on the cusp of manhood and is learning his duty as a gentleman—"a figure necessary to social cohesion, justice, and peace in any regime imaginable." His quest to exonerate Lucas does, indeed, result in justice, but Chick is deeply disturbed by the hatred he has seen exposed in his community—so disturbed that he is on the verge of renouncing his identity as a part of the community in which he was born and raised.[9] Thus he is "instructed" by his uncle Gavin who engages, in a series of exchanges between the two, in the "pacification of Chick's troubled spirit, of his shame and outrage ..." while prodding him toward a deeper understanding of Southern history and the importance of preserving "the moral and political independence of the South." The crux of Gavin's message is that justice will come for Southern blacks, but only when they are ready to assume full responsibility for their equality. Just as importantly, the solution to the racial injustice of the Jim Crow system (an injustice which every thoughtful white man concedes, at least privately) must not come from external, coercive forces, but from within the cultural resources of the South herself.

Some years prior to "Text and Context ..." Bradford had already written an extensive essay on Faulkner's struggle to find a morally acceptable position on desegregation. That essay, "Faulkner, James Baldwin, and the South,"[10] took its impetus from a piece by black writer James Baldwin, entitled "Faulkner and Segregation," which had been included in Baldwin's *Nobody Knows My Name* (1961).[11] Baldwin's quarrel with Faulkner was provoked by a statement made by the latter in an interview in the *Reporter*, a liberal news magazine,

---

9   See *Intruder in the* Dust (New York: Random House, 1948), 194-195.

10   The essay was published in the *Georgia Review*, vol. 20 (Winter 1966), 431-433.

11   "Faulkner and Segregation" had originally been published in *The Partisan Review* (Fall 1956), 568-573.

with the British journalist Russell Howe. [12] On that occasion, after being pressed by Howe about whether he (Faulkner) would continue to maintain a conciliatory position if Mississippi were faced with a federal attempt to force the state's schools to desegregate, Faulkner stated, "As long as there's a middle road, all right, I'll be on it. But if it came to fighting, I'd fight for Mississippi against the United States, even if it meant going into the streets and shooting negros." Naturally, the remarks caused something of a scandal in certain quarters, and Baldwin was not alone in asking (in this case several years after the fact): "Why—and how—does one move from the middle of the road where one was aiding negroes—into the streets—to shoot them?" Bradford, in his response to Baldwin's query, emphasizes at some length his conviction that Baldwin failed to understand—was perhaps incapable of understanding—Faulkner's sense of the communal bond or "corporate spirit" that he shared with his fellow Mississippians, white and black alike. While his comment about "shooting negroes in the street" (if he wasn't misquoted) was no doubt rash, his underlying meaning is the real issue. He had on a number of occasions in those years expressed his willingness to support desegregation, he also stated more than once that such a dramatic change in the status quo must arise only out of a consensual embrace of such change on the part of black and white Southern leaders. Any resort to coercion by outside forces could only lead to long term distrust between the races.

How could Baldwin, Bradford asks, possibly understand the kind of communal bonds that Faulkner cherished? Having grown up in Harlem in the midst of thousands of deracinated blacks, how could he have understood what it means to find one's identity rooted in many generations sharing the same sense of place, bound together by innumerable ties of sanguinity and custom? The kind of community championed by Faulkner depends for its survival on constant "restoration and renewal through adjustment to new circumstances and ... resistance against any and all attempts to pull it up by the roots, to break off utterly from the past and start afresh."

---

12   The interview was published in the *Reporter* on March 22, 1956, and shortly thereafter in the London *Sunday Times*.

In Bradford's understanding, following Faulkner, the endurance of the social order depends ultimately upon the "stewardship of place." It is this stewardship that Gavin Stevens sought to instill in Chick Mallison.

If I have digressed at some length on the "color line" in Faulkner, it is not simply that the fallout from his remarks in the *Reporter* interview offer us a vivid sense of the enormous external pressure being exerted on the South even as early as the late 1940s when Faulkner was composing *Intruder,* and how acutely Faulkner, both as a man and as a writer, felt that pressure as the desegregation drama unfolded and threatened violently to disrupt the by then fragile Southern solidarity. It is also because Bradford's own response to Baldwin anticipates some of the views he expresses in his 1992 essay "The Great Enterprise"[13] (Chap. 16), which the reader of this volume will find of great interest on the matter of the vast expansion of Faulkner studies in academe in the latter half of the twentieth century. Indeed, so voluminous had the "Faulkner industry" become by 1992 that it had become the engine of American literary criticism, producing dozens of new volumes for the academic presses each year, volumes written for the most part by critics with little or no familiarity with the Southern *habitus.* Thus began to appear studies on feminist issues in Faulkner, deconstructive criticism of Faulkner, neo-Marxist readings of Faulkner, and, of course, endless analyses of racial issues in Faulkner. Virtually all of these publications (written primarily to promote ideological affinities or to garner tenure) were, as Bradford so memorably notes, were "readings ... infected by an ahistorical cosmopolitanism." Such cosmopolitan critics, like James Baldwin, are necessarily rootless individuals whose "ideas concerning the present political value of literature overwhelm almost every other consideration." Bradford laudably dismisses most of this criticism as "trendy nonsense" of importance only "to a decadent ruling class." But this is not to say that he relegates all of the criticism of those years to the same dung heap. Some few volumes he finds worthy of praise, including Daniel Hoffman's

---

13   "The Great Enterprise" was published in *the Sewanee Review* (Fall 1992), Vol. 100, 700-705.

Faulkner's Country Matters: Folklore and Fable in Yoknapatawpha (1989), which recognizes what so many Faulkner critics overlook—the novelist's immersion in the oral traditions of Mississippi and the South, his devotion "to memory and the old task of the poet to refine and transmit his particular culture in rehearsing its myths."[14]

Finally, we hope that the readers of this volume will find, as we have, that Mel Bradford is among the most reliable of guides through the sometimes intricate byways of Faulkner's Yoknapatawpha. Most importantly, what he helps us to see is Faulkner's profound recreation of that mysterious, sometimes tragic, sometimes comic, all-encompassing order that we all inhabit, the order that Bradford describes (in Chap. 10) as "arrangement of providentially assigned roles" that demands of us "submission, courtesy, and mutual respect"—and, above all, "a sense of transcendent pity."

Jack Trotter

October 2023

---

14   This is Bradford's paraphrase of Hoffman's point, 704.

1.

Faulkner's "Tall Men"[15]

No group of characters in the Yoknapatawpha Cycle offers more insight into the human qualities which Faulkner most admires than do his yeoman farmers. To this group belong most of Faulkner's white male characters who are not Snopeses, Sartorises, or white trash. To them he has given a local habitation and a name. Many of them, according to *The Hamlet*[16] and *The Town,*[17] are, as late as 1943, still living in the wooded hills and narrow valleys above Frenchman's Bend. They are "the tall men," the descendants of the original white settlers of the region.

Like their forefathers they are "independent men"[18] and remain almost unaffected in the mid-twentieth century by the coming of industrialism and the new capitalism to the South—indeed live beyond the reach of these powers and resist their influence. Proud, yet not greedy, they remain self-sufficient. They are clannish, keep to themselves, regulate their own lives, and resent all unnecessary

---

15　Originally published in *The South Atlantic Quarterly*, Vol. LXI (Duke University Press, 1962), 29-39.

16　*The Hamlet* (New York: Random House, 1940), 4-5.

17　*The Town* (New York: Random House, 1957), 316-317. [*The Hamlet* and *The Town* are the first two volumes of the so-called "Snopes trilogy"; followed by *The Mansion* (New York: Random House, 1959), ed.]

18　*The Big Woods* (New York: Random House, 1955), is a collection of Faulkner's short stories, generally regarded as among his best. [Ed.]

limitations upon their liberty by government or intrusion; and they are willing to pay the price of liberty. These Mississippi "tall men" belong in spirit to the republic of independent farmers into which Thomas Jefferson had hoped the United States would develop. Their counterparts are still to be found among the farm folk of upper New England and the Middle West. In the fiction of William Faulkner these men represent a moral as well as a social and economic condition; and to understand what he finds admirable in them and how they, according to him, came to develop the qualities he admires is to understand a great deal about the moral norms which govern his fable of southern history.

For some reason critics of Faulkner's fiction have generally ignored the role played in that fiction by these "tall men." Their oversight is a repetition of that made by many interpreters of southern society. Frederick Law Olmsted in his *A Journey in the Back Country* (1860) classified the white rural population of the South into two groups: the planters and the "poor whites." This misconception of southern society is still current, as is evident in the writings of Max Lerner, Ray Billington, Henry Steele Commager, and others. It should have been forever laid to rest by F. L. Owsley's *Plain Folk of the Old South*.[19] Professor Owsley shows clearly that the majority of the white population of the antebellum South were neither indigents nor large planters. Most of that population lived on small farms of two to five hundred acres, owned their land, but had few or no slaves. Professor Owsley's summary of the character of these plain folk as a group serves as the best possible preface to a study of the role their fictional counterparts play in the Yoknapatawpha Cycle.

According to Professor Owsley, "Relatively few of the plain folk seem to have had a desire to become wealthy. Their ambition was to acquire land and other property sufficient to give them and their children a sense of security and well-being, to be 'good livers' and have 'something saved for a rainy day' as they would put it."[20] Dr.

_____

19   *Plain Folk of the Old South* (Baton Rouge: Louisiana State University Press, 1949). [Walter Lynwood Fleming Lectures on Southern History series]

20   *Plain Folk*, 133-134.

Owsley goes on to describe their patriarchal society, to discuss their love of hunting, their preference for wooded hills over plains and big valleys, their religious character, their emphasis on the art of living, and especially their pride and self-respect. He carefully distinguishes them from the shiftless, spineless trash with whom they are often confused and makes their self-respect and sense of honor the basis of his distinction. To them Professor Owsley attributes the economic recovery of the South after the Civil War. His book depicts the "plain folk" as representatives of a mean between the extremes of aggressiveness and passivity, as occupants of a middle ground between the big planters (and would-be big planters) and the relatively small residue of human waste at the bottom of the southern social scale.

Faulkner attributes precisely the same qualities to his "tall men." They are not men with a private dream or design like Sutpen,[21] Carothers McCaslin, or Flem Snopes. On the other hand they are not utterly passive, shiftless, or fatalistic like Wash Jones in *Absalom, Absalom!* or Quentin's father, Jason Compson III, in *The Sound and the Fury*.[22] In themselves they maintain a balance of "pride and humility" (key words in all of Faulkner's stories about hunters and woodsmen). They are not subject to the machinations of a Flem Snopes because they are not often governed by those particular impulses which would play them into the hands of a Snopes. Unwilling to let the Leviathan State assume responsibility for their fate, they remain in modern times unaffected by that collective loss of the sense of a personal responsibility which Faulkner treats symbolically in *Requiem for a Nun*[23] in his discussion of the growth of Jefferson's courthouse.[24] They live much in the woods, love hunting and good whiskey. Though they dislike the intrusion of strangers or

---

21   Thomas Sutpen is a central character in Faulkner's *Absalom, Absalom!* (New York: Random House, 1936).

22   *The Sound and the Fury* (New York: Jonathan Cape and Harrison Smith, 1929).

23   *Requiem for a Nun* (New York: Random House, 1951).

24   In *Requiem* and elsewhere Faulkner's descriptions of the Jefferson courthouse suggest that it is a symbolic *microcosm*—not simply of the fictional world of Yoknapa-tawpha but of southern civilization. In *Requiem*, the courthouse is described at some

government officials in their affairs, they are otherwise hospitable. In the "roadless, almost pathless, almost perpendicular hill country" above Frenchman's Bend they build their cabins of two rooms split by a dog-run, raise cotton in the bottom, corn on the ridges, and large families.

Among them, more than among any other group of people in the Yoknapatawpha Cycle, old ways survive. Their forefathers had come into Yoknapatawpha County from Culloden Moor and the Carolinas through the Tennessee mountains southwestward, "by stages marked by the bearing and raising of a generation of children, bringing little with them but their weapons, dogs, children, and hymn books." What they brought and what they acquire, they keep. In the 1940's Faulkner has them still speaking a little Gaelic and just as clannish as ever. He also has most of them living on the very land where their forefathers first settled after the Indian removal. After over one hundred years they remain "uxorious, prolific," old-time Protestants and old-time Jeffersonian Democrats.

Despite the lack of "glamor" in their traditional life, Faulkner recognizes that theirs is the oldest southern tradition, that of the frontier, a tradition like that of "the old people," the Indians they supplanted (for whom Faulkner has great admiration). Much of the best of the planter tradition—of the Sartorises, Compsons, and De Spains—to whose code Faulkner criticism has justifiably given so much attention, can be identified with the patriarchal tradition of the "plain folk." (Professor Owsley furnishes historical evidence for this identification.) And as *Sartoris* (1929), *The Hamlet,* "The Tall Men," and certain of Faulkner's hunting stories show, the upheavals of Civil War, Reconstruction, and modern times did not impair or destroy the continuity of the tradition of the "plain folk" as they did that of a large percentage of the planter aristocracy.

---

length: its construction in the antebellum era; its destruction by fire by the Union army during the War Between the States; and its eventual rebuilding. See "Act I: The Court-house (A Name for the City)," 9-49 [Ed.]

Which characters in the Yoknapatawpha Cycle belong to this group? In *The Town*[25] Faulkner gives a list of piney woods, upland clans: Frazier and Muir, Turpin and Murray, Haley and McCallum. The McCallums epitomize these people. Like most of the "tall men," they are of Gaelic extraction. They are a family of men; when one of them marries, his wife presents him with a few sons and then quietly dies. By the time the events in "The Tall Men" take place, they have been living in Yoknapatawpha County for over one hundred years.[26] Like their neighbors they are neither rich nor poor by the standards of Yoknapatawpha County (although they are better off than most of the "plain folk"). They are hunters; indeed, their home is almost a glorified hunting camp. Large, masculine, unvarnished men, they are nevertheless openly, unselfconsciously affectionate with one another. They are what is rare in Faulkner's fiction, a completely happy family, beholden to no man, asking no one's help or advice. Open, friendly, and generous with their time and means, they do not defer to the names of Sartoris, De Spain, or Compson; yet they are on friendly, almost familiar terms with these families.

In *Sartoris* we are told that the young Sartoris twins, John and Bayard, were given an important part of their early education in the house, fields, and woods of the patriarch of the clan, Anse McCallum. The boys, according to Bayard, spent the happiest days of their youth with Anse and his six sons. To the McCallums Bayard flees after he, with his wild driving, has killed his grandfather; he again hunts with them as he did when a boy; but now their world offers him no solace, only sharpens his sense of guilt.[27] The world of the McCallums [has become] Bayard's paradise lost. This section of *Sartoris* sets off his spiritual sickness and guilt in sharp relief and poignant isolation against the homely idyll which is the life of the

---

25 *Requiem*, 316-317.

26 "The Tall Men." *Collected Stories of William* Faulkner (New York: Random House, 1950), 45-61.

27 *Sartoris* (New York: Random House, 1929), 177. *Sartoris* was an abridged edition of the novel Faulkner originally wrote under the title *Flags in the Dust*, which was eventually published in its entirety by Random House in 1973, 11 years after the author's death.

McCallums. His lost and desperate behavior is best understood in terms of the tension which the novel articulates between the new Jefferson and the timeless dignity, simplicity, and repose of the McCallums' world.

In "The Tall Men" we see the McCallums most clearly. Nowhere in Faulkner's fiction is his tone more affirmative than it is in this story. Old Anse has been dead fifteen years, and Buddy, his youngest son (and the one most like him), now presides over the clan. Buddy has, since the events recorded in *Sartoris*, married, had twin sons, and lost his wife. Now in the McCallum house are the six brothers, sons of Old Anse, grandsons of the McCallum who first settled in the county; and Buddy's two boys, about twenty years old by this time (*ca.* 1940). Yet to a remarkable extent Old Anse, in the minds of his sons and grandsons, is still a living presence in the house he had built in 1866.

By 1940 the house has grown, but its outlines remain the same. Its basic structure is that of the typical split house of the "plain folk," two rooms under one roof but completely separated by a dog-run set between them. The pattern of life on the McCallum place has outwardly changed but remains unchanged in essentials. Now the McCallums have cattle, not cotton; they refused to plough their crop under and would not let the government tell them how much to plant and guarantee their price. An emblem, a visible token of the continuity of their family's life, is the house in which they live. In it the present rests on and grows out of the past—the additions have been built on and around the original house. The very appearance of the house and the fence around it (rambling and paintless but stout and substantial) suggests the character of the people who live in it. Even the striking physical resemblance they bear one another betokens the remarkable unity and continuity of spirit which bind together the McCallums, living and dead.

"The Tall Men" depicts the experience of a young draft board investigator who is taken out to the McCallums' farm by the old county marshal. He has come to serve a warrant on Anse and Lucius McCallum, Buddy's twin sons; the McCallums had ignored notices from the draft board and failed to register with it. The young man has come up from Jackson, convinced that the McCallums belong to the class of people who are burdens on the state but no help to it in time of trouble. He has a low opinion of the rural population of the Mississippi of his day, most of whom he feels have gladly become wards of the state, the WPA[28], and everything that came with it. It is his opinion that these people are completely dishonorable. The marshal's real purpose in taking the young man out to the McCallums is educational. He knows what the outsider is thinking, knows what the McCallums will do. He wants the young federal agent to meet the McCallums, see the twin boys leave for the Army, and understand why they had misinterpreted or ignored the notices from the draft board. In a sense the draft investigator may be taken as a representative "outsider" and the marshal as a chorus character— the voice of Faulkner instructing the outside world concerning one facet of his microcosmos.

When the marshal and the federal agent arrive, they discover that Buddy McCallum had earlier that day mangled his leg in a hammer mill. They enter the house, and the younger man is astonished at his own reaction to the McCallums. Buddy is in bed, his brothers and sons gathered around him; the federal investigator is awed by the "presence" of these men. They seem to him "giants" (though only Buddy and his sons have Old Anse's height). Their "stature" is a quality of character which their physical presence, their house, and [their] farm seem to radiate. It transcends (and is foreign to) that variety of virtue which the draft investigator has come to reprimand them for violating.

After the marshal explains why he and the young man have come, Buddy (who had been much decorated for gallantry in World War I) instructs his sons to proceed immediately to Memphis and there enlist in the Army, preferably in his old regiment. He tells them to obey the orders and their officers and adds, "Remember

---

28 The Works Progress Administration, created as part of the New Deal in 1935 during the presidency of Franklin Roosevelt. [Ed.]

your name and don't take nothing from no man."[29] The boys do not delay but "approach the bed and bend down and kiss their father on the mouth and turn as one and leave the room." The federal agent protests feebly against these proceedings. Buddy replies that no war has started to his knowledge, that he misunderstood the messages from the draft board, and that recent experiences have made him hesitant about signing papers from the government. This further confuses the man from Jackson; but as the boys leave, he and the marshal notice that the doctor is about to amputate Buddy's leg (without anesthetics) and the marshal leads the younger man, who is now resigned to his helplessness, out into the dog-run.

They have only a short time to wait before a carefully wrapped bundle is passed out to them. The marshal takes it and asks the younger man to help him bury Buddy's leg. They go up to the family graveyard, another symbol of the continuity in the life of this family; and there the laconic old marshal explains to the befuddled federal agent (and, indirectly, to us) what he has seen and felt. The marshal, as he digs in the spot where Buddy himself will eventually be buried, tells the story of Old Anse McCallum, of what Old Anse had learned from life and of what he in turn had taught his boys. The marshal juxtaposes his discussion of the McCallums and their tradition with remarks on the weak character of modern men, and does it in such a way as to make obvious why in his eyes the McCallums are extraordinary men.

He remarks, "We moderns have slipped our backbone" and have "invented so many alphabets and rules and recipes that we are lost."[30] In other words, modern man has forgotten that he is an individual, a morally accountable being and that as such, he is greater than the law. He has come to misunderstand his own nature, and the results are Horace Benbow's Gloucester-like meditation on man's helplessness in *Sartoris*[31] and the remarks of Quentin's father, Jason Compson III, about the illusion of free will in *The*

---

29 "The Tall Men," 53.

30 "The Tall Men," 59.

31 *Sartoris*, 177.

Sound and the Fury. A further result, the marshal implies, is the coming of the welfare state, symbolized in the story by the WPA. The McCallums value life, value it too much to take a WPA check or an agricultural subsidy and thereby deny responsibility for their own fate. They feel that life is valuable only on certain terms, valuable only to independent men. For the marshal they are the most natural of men, embodiments of a balance between pride and humility, of an undivided sensibility.

Once the marshal has finished his story of the McCallums and their dealings with the federal government, the young federal agent (we suppose) understands why they didn't sign the registration papers sent to them by the draft board. Government papers for them had come to signify, since the coming of the New Deal to Yoknapatawpha County, man's surrender of responsibility for himself, his loss of personal importance, honor, self-respect—"backbone." Old Anse had learned from the Civil War and its aftermath [both] pride and humility; he had learned humility from defeat; and also from defeat and his struggle during Reconstruction times he had learned to rebuild his life, had realized the necessity of pride, honor and responsible behavior in life if it is to remain meaningful. According to the marshal, this perspective on life is what Old Anse had passed on to his descendants; and they had proved out his teachings by following them, by farming his fields and hunting his woods.

The McCallums occasionally appear elsewhere in Faulkner's fiction; though they are usually in the background, their counterparts are scattered throughout the Yoknapatawpha Cycle. Jackson Fentry in "Tomorrow," the Griers in "Shall Not Perish," and Mr. Ernest in "Race at Morning" are "plain folk."[32] Byron Bunch, the humble and persistent suitor of Lena Grove in *Light in August*[33] is one of them.

---

32 "Shall Not Perish" is included in the *Collected Stories of William Faulkner*, 101-115; "Tomorrow" is one of the stories in *Knight's Gambit* (1940); and "Race at Morning" may be found in *Big Woods* (1955) as well as in the *Uncollected Stories* (New York: Random House, 1979), ed. Joseph Blotner.

33 *Light in August* (New York: Harrison Smith and Robert Haas, 1932).

Another is the convict in *The Old Man*,[34] who is uncomplaining in his misfortune but conscious "of his good name, his responsibility ..., his honor in doing what was asked of him, his pride in being able to do it." All of these characters are, like the McCallums, animated by a mixture of pride and humility. They are humble, self-effacing, independent, unselfconsciously virtuous, responsible, taciturn, and self-respecting. Though they play an inconspicuous part in the life around them, they are never merely the pawns of circumstance. There is a "vein of iron" in their make-up that bears up well under test.

They play a role among their people like that played in earlier times by Uncle Buck and Uncle Buddy McCaslin. Buck and Buddy are most interesting because they identify themselves with the McCallums and their kind. Their father, the Sutpen-like autocrat Carothers McCaslin, had like Governor Compson acquired a large tract of the old Chickasaw lands. He was a man with a design, a dream of empire; and he left his twin sons (who are up in years when we first see them in *The Unvanquished*[35]) the wreck of that design. Buck and Buddy repudiate their father's ruthless ways. Into their hands falls a vast tract of land, a huge unfinished mansion, and a nondescript mob of Negro slaves—some of whom have McCaslin blood in their veins. Buck and Buddy refuse to live in the great unfinished house and instead construct for themselves with their own hands a simple two-room cabin with a dog-run, just like the house built by Anse McCallum in 1866. They live simply, lack all pretension; but they regard the land and the slaves as a responsibility, and in that sense they accept their patrimony. They "belong to it." They treat their slaves as charges, not things; and when one earns his freedom with hard labor and responsible behavior, they give it to him. The others, they realize, would suffer terribly if given their freedom and therefore must remain under "fatherly" control. They are made to do just

---

34   *The Old Man* is one of two interwoven novellas in *The Wild Palms* (New York: Random House, 1939). The quote used here may be found on p. 166 of the 1939 edition. Some more recent editions have been released under the title *If I Forget Thee, Jerusalem*.

35   *The Unvanquished* (New York; Random House, 1938).

enough to keep the plantation on its feet.[36] Buck and Buddy, knowing that the Book says that the sins of the father shall descend to the generations of his sons, take the responsibility for what Carothers has done. As Faulkner put it elsewhere, " ... they did the best they could"; in contrast Ike McCaslin (the son of one and nephew of the other), when faced with the tainted patrimony and responsibility for it, rationalizes, " ... this is bad and I will withdraw from it."[37]

But Buck and Buddy do more than accept inherited responsibilities. They take on new ones. Not content to espouse revolutionary ideas on slavery, they bring together their Negroes, bond and free, and the wretchedly poor among the white farmers of their region into a co-operative agricultural enterprise and thus come, like patriarchs of old, to see after the well-being of a considerable segment of the population of Yoknapatawpha County. Their object is to help these people help themselves. John Sartoris finds out how beloved they are by all the poor folk of the county when he is trying to organize a regiment in 1861. Unless he agrees to take Uncle Buddy with him, he discovers, he will not go to Virginia as colonel of the regiment.

The McCaslin twins do have a dream, a design; but it is not a private one. Drusilla[38] tells young Bayard Sartoris that John Sartoris is superior to Sutpen because his dream is not just "Sartoris," not just for himself.[39] Unfortunately, tragically, his dream is a bit too much "Sartoris." But the McCaslin twins seek nothing in pride, seek no more than they need for themselves. As patriarchs they must keep control over large numbers of people and a vast acreage if they are to fulfill their responsibilities. But their dress, habits of mind, dwelling

---

36   *The Unvanquished*, 45-46.

37   *Faulkner in the University* (University of Virginia Press: Charlottesville, Va, 1959), 39, 246. This book is basically the transcript of some 37 "conferences" hosted by the University while Faulkner was writer-in-residence there in 1957-58. The conferences were essentially forums for students and faculty, who were thus afforded the opportunity to ask the author questions about his life and work.

38   Drusilla, or "Cousin Drusilla," is a relation of the Sartoris family, and plays a prominent role in *The Unvanquished*.

39   *The Unvanquished*, 169.

place, and way of living make it clear that they have dissociated themselves from the planter class, or at least from certain qualities which they identify with it, especially excessive pride and greed.

Perhaps the McCaslin twins' attitude toward the land best distinguishes them and their approach to life from the Sutpens, Compsons, De Spains, and their own father: "They believed that the land did not belong to people but the people belonged to the land and that the earth would permit them to live on and out of it and use it only so long as they behaved."[40] That is to say, they believed in patriarchy, believed that man's proper role in the world is defined, as Hyatt Waggoner has stated, in the concept of "what the church calls stewardship."[41] They believed that men belong to the circumstances which confront them, that land and property are a fief from God, given by Him to some in order that they may fulfill responsibilities in pride (at being chosen and in meeting tests) and in humility (as servants). To live out of the land and to use it in a spirit of stewardship is to "behave."

Although Ike McCaslin fails to live up to the measure of his father, Buck, and his uncle, it is his life (as recounted in *The Bear* and "Delta Autumn"[42]) which explains most fully how the McCaslins and other "tall men" come to be what they are. Ike's education in the woods in the hunt (for him a parable of all life) is representative. From it he and all of his kind "acquire the will and hardihood to endure and the humility and skill to survive."[43] From the hunt they learn that bravery is necessary, that the untested life is shameful, and that shame is worse than death. In the presence of the "sombre,

---

40 *The Unvanquished*, 45.

41 *William Faulkner: From Jefferson to the World* (Lexington, Ky: University of Kentucky Press, 1959), 206.

42 Both *The Bear* and "Delta Autumn" are included in *Go Down, Moses* (New York: Random House, 1942).

43 *Go Down, Moses*, 191.

impenetrable…,"[44] brooding and ineffable forest they are put in mind of their dependent status, their finitude. Their experience with nature as farmers reinforces this awareness.

Others among Faulkner's characters who are not hunters, woodsmen, or pine-hill farmers have chastening experiences which work upon their inner selves just as the pattern of life inherited and practiced by the "tall men" works upon them. From such tests Dilsey and Chick Mallison[45] emerge as completely admirable characters. Yet no other recognizable group or class of people in Faulkner's fiction so completely embodies that balance of pride and humility, assertiveness and passive submission which Faulkner accepts as the norm for responsible human behavior as do the "tall men." In them Faulkner finds a usable past, a tradition among his people with which he can measure other traditions, southern or otherwise—a pattern of life and a perspective on life which explains what is for him the South's tragic history.

Perhaps they do not play too large a role in the Yoknapatawpha Cycle, but it is easy to explain why they do not. Faulkner's vision is essentially tragic. He affirms that set of values to which he subscribes by creating images of a world devoid of those values. The "tall men," about whom he has told us enough for us to determine what he admires in them, are in his fiction emblems of a moral condition. What they mean to him is not what they would mean to an cconomist or a sociologist, who would probably identify them as "barriers to regional progress." But for Faulkner the pattern of life which the "tall men" follow (a pattern which, he recognizes, has as its consequence their belonging to a social and economic subdivision of their own country's population) represents a moral alternative to both the withdrawn passivity and sense of hopelessness and the aggressive, empire-building will-to-power which animate most of his characters. If the values which the McCallums and Buck and

---

44 *Go Down, Moses*, 196.

45 Charles "Chick" Malison, Jr. is at once a character and the narrator of a number of chapters in *The Town* (New York: Random House, 1957); Dilsey Gibson is a character in *The Sound and the Fury* (1929).

Buddy McCaslin personify had utterly prevailed in the history of Yoknapatawpha County, Faulkner would have found in it very little material for his art. As Robert Penn Warren declared in a lecture at Vanderbilt University some years ago, " ... there is no literature in heaven."

2.

Faulkner and the Great White Father[46]

"Lo!" is one of Faulkner's Indian stories. Its most obvious implications link it with the discussions in "Delta Autumn," "The Bear," the narrative sections of *Requiem for a Nun*, "The Old People," and *Big Woods* of the difference between the "first Americans" and the white men who pushed them aside. In it, as in these other stories, Faulkner uses the quiet and organic Indian culture as a foil for the aggressions and prideful dreams of the white man. Here, as elsewhere, he suggests that the Indian is perhaps the more civilized and more tolerant, the Anglo-Saxon/Celt the more adolescent and self-delusive of the two cultures. His perspective on the significance of their disparity is like that developed by another Southern writer, Caroline Gordon, in her novel, *Green Centuries*.

The story has also another theme, that of the relationship of an abstract and ideologically rigid central authority to the heterogeneous collection of subcultures which it is supposed to represent and govern. Much of the humor of this story follows as a consequence of the official commitment of this central authority to the idea that all its people "are the same" and the admission in practice of its spokesman, the President of the United States, that nothing of the kind is, in fact, true.

---

46   This essay was first published in *Louisiana Studies* 3, no. 4 (Winter 1964), 323-329.

"Lo!" has been much neglected by the critics—perhaps because, unlike its counterparts, "A Courtship," and "Red Leaves," [47] it does not lend itself to lengthy and sanctimonious moralizing about the perils of "social injustice." Like "Race at Morning" and "The Tall Men," it has a burden which runs against the modern grain.

"Lo!" is set in times preceding the Indian removal from Mississippi: the events in the story occur not long after the earliest attempts of the white man to settle in and acquire the old Chickasaw nation. The occasion of the action in the story is the difficulty which ensues from the difference between the Indian and the white attitudes towards the lands in question and toward their possession. The protagonist, Francis Weddel (or Vidal) the half-French/half-Chickasaw patriarch or "Man" of the nation has a valid and irrevocable title to several hundred square miles of territory on one side of what is probably the Yazoo River. Though the old chief does in his own way own the land in the name of all his people and recognizes the importance to the Chickasaw of the preservation of their title to as much of that land as they will need for their own purposes, he does not regard ownership as a means of self-aggrandizement or ego gratification. As Faulkner puts it elsewhere, he holds it in "fee simple" from a bountiful providence and is willing that white men share in the ownership and use of [that part of it which] his people do not need. But he comes to recognize that there is a "restlessness" or a madness about these white men which drives them to want to "possess" the land absolutely unto themselves. Because of such restlessness a white man had bought from him a small section of his people's land—which included the only ford across a river in a three-hundred-mile stretch—and then denied the Indians access to that ford unless they paid toll. The result of this white man's peculiar and (from the Indian's point of view) indefensible behavior was his murder by Weddel's nephew. The Indian agent, who to the Chickasaw represented the great chief or "White Father" in Washington, inquired into the murder. Upon his inquiry the entire Indian nation packed its bags and set out to

---

47   "Red Leaves" is an Indian story set among the Chickasaw, first published in 1930. "A Courtship (1948) is Faulkner's last Indian tale. Both are included in *Collected Stories of William Faulkner* (New York: Random House, 1950), pt. 3: "The Wilderness." [Ed.]

Washington to receive at the hands of the great chief the kind of personal and final judgment which their patriarchal worldview had accustomed them to expect and accept.

The results are hilarious. The population of the eastern seaboard is terrified. The Indians come by the thousands: Silent, formal, mannerly, and exasperating. They pay innumerable unannounced visits to farms, villages, and towns and come finally to camp all over the capital city, to sleep in entrance ways, hunt deer on foot with knives, cook and pitch tents on lawns, and walk about in groups with their top hats on and their pantaloons folded under their arms. Although Weddel holds no brief with the madness of white men and understands his nephew's anger at the toll gate, he regrets the murder and prefers that his people be indulgent with the vagaries and peculiarities of their restless neighbors; and he wants to submit himself and his nephew good-humoredly and respectfully to "my great white friend and chief [who] has removed [from his presence] the face of every enemy save death ... ." [48] As he sees the matter, when he put himself under the authority of the United States government, he became directly responsible to the President to see to it that his people do not "slay white men like a confounded Cherokee or Creek,"[49] but instead recognize the greed and obsession which the white men cannot help. Though he feels no particular guilt at his nephew's deed (only impatience with his ignorance of the whites), he is a gentleman, sensitive of the dignity of his overlord and friend, concerned for (as one of his tribe puts it) the President's "honor" in this matter.

Therefore, to save everyone's face, he feels that he must come all the way from Mississippi to recognize officially the President's authority to judge his nephew and thus reaffirm the Chickasaw's relationship to that authority. But abstract justice or a mere document of exoneration for the young man he cannot accept; it would be an insult to "the People." Government, as his culture understands it, is the product of the traditional wisdom personified

---

48 *Collected Stories*, 401.

49 *Collected Stories*, 395-396.

in the leadership of reverend men. So to Washington he goes, with all his kin and connection. In a matter which involves something as serious as the reaffirmation of patriarchal authority, he expects the President's judgment to be accompanied by some ceremony.

The antagonist in the story, the well-meaning but only half comprehending President (who vaguely suggests Andrew Jackson) is both exasperated and helpless at the Indian "invasion" of the capital and its environs. He learns quickly of the events which brought it on and of the interview with Weddel that he will have to hold to lift the siege; but he puts off this interview for as long as he can in the hope that the Indians will simply go away so that he can avoid an encounter he does not k now how to conduct. Finally, as inconvenience for all the citizens of Washington increases and as outcries of protest at the continued Chickasaw invasion pour in from the nearby countryside, he surrenders. Arrangements are made for a meeting in a cabinet member's house; and the story's theme becomes apparent.

Weddel and his nephew appear and the events which led to the killing are rehearsed. The old chief asks the President to declare if his "foolish boy" is a murderer (that is to say, is guilty of a serious crime in this killing). There is no question in the Chickasaw's mind but that some small punishment will be imposed upon his nephew. But no! The President writes out a letter of official exoneration. However, under these informal circumstances and in this setting Weddel will not be satisfied. The ceremony must be held in the Capitol itself, in the place where official government business is transacted (the counterpart of the Indian council house); and it must be done with a fitting and proper ritual. The President finally obliges with a parade, a guard of troops, a long and sonorous reading from Petrarch's Latin verse, and a roll of cannon. The heads of the Indian nation are present; and with this pomp, they are satisfied and return home.

In these two scenes and throughout the story Faulkner emphasizes the differences that distinguish the white from the Indian culture. Both Weddel and the President acknowledge them, though the latter at the same time pays appropriate lip service to the uniformitarian Jacobin abstractions that are part of the political doctrine of the

New Republic. He tries to tell Weddel that he has no power over Congress to make its chambers available for the presentation of his judgment; this nonsense the old Indian wryly refuses to believe. The President then assures the Chickasaw that it makes no difference in his handling of this matter that Weddel and his people are Indians and that to his government "my Indian and my white people are the same." [50] This statement produces only amusement in the half-breed chief and a polite and yet condescending reiteration of his disarming acknowledgement, "we are but Indians."[51] He wants "to act like these people believe the Indians ought to act"; [52] but he is aware of how tenuous and artificial is the relationship of the Chickasaw nation to the United States government. He is also aware that "you never know what they [white people] are going to do next" [53] and so must deal patiently with them and as indulgently with their political as with their economic delusions. Therefore he insists on the ceremony.

After Weddel goes home the difficulties seem to have been resolved; but then in the following autumn, the President receives a letter from Mississippi, a letter whose "bland words seem to explode one by one in his comprehension like musketry." It is from Francis Weddel. Another white man has come among the Chickasaw who "after the curious and restless fashion of white men" is unwilling to "hunt in peace" in "God's Forest" but is instead obsessed with the idea of owning this ford ... . [54] The hot-headed nephew has behaved predictably and taken the aforementioned white man for a swim in the river—from which only the nephew returned. Therefore, the letter continues, the people have once again bestirred themselves northward. With this news, the President's commitment to the idea that all people are the same completely collapses. Troops are dispatched to forestall the visit. Orders are given to shoot, if necessary, every horse, mule, and ox in the possession of the

---

50 *Collected Stories*, 397.

51 *Collected Stories*, 396.

52 *Collected Stories*, 383.

53 *Collected Stories*, 383.

54 *Collected Stories*, 401.

Indians. Patriarchy proves to be too heavy a burden on the Chief Executive's shoulders and he issues another absolutely illegal decree (now in his own name and not in his role as legal head of state) that the ford may no longer be sold, given away, or leased by or from the Indians, and that anyone who crosses it into their territory (or anyone of them who leaves the same) does so at his own peril. The abstraction "The United States" is dispensed with and in its place stands the inevitable figure of the responsible man who, in rejecting his patriarchal authority over some of his people, in effect performs it with regard to the rest. On the basis available to him under a law which has as its premise the assumption that all his people are the same, a law made in a chamber where a new breed of statesmen are mindful only of a "high dream of destiny superior to the injustice of events and the folly of mankind," [55] he cannot meaningfully relate his authority to his Indian charges. Nothing in the arrangement of responsibilities which he has acquired through election, nothing in the legal machinery of the new republic, is properly constituted to enable him to deal in fairness and justice with these people. For its basis is uniformitarian, and its substance not readily adaptable to the fact of human difference. However, for the Indians only his personal judgment of questions which arise in their midst will suffice—if he is to inject himself into such questions at all.

The implication of the story—that the approach of the government in Washington (and some aspects of the ideology upon which it rests) to the distinctive cultural and social units under its authority is defective—remains plain. It is further implied that in the government of a huge and varied "nation" (to a degree a misnomer when applied to the United States), it would be best to follow the Roman example and leave to the distinct societies of which it is composed the administration of a practical, local justice—a justice mindful of the socio-cultural facts which locally prevail. If it becomes necessary for the federal government to act, it should do so with such facts in mind—as does the President in this story in his exasperated and extemporaneous gestures on behalf of order.

---

55   *Collected Stories*, 399.

Those familiar with *Intruder in the Dust* will not find the affirmation in "Lo!" of Faulkner's faith in the wisdom of genuine communities surprising; neither will the Faulkner critics who have studied his version of American history or his teleology be surprised at the scorn there suggested for the folly of schemes to impose a "foreign" and arbitrary pattern of living upon organically developed and historically rooted cultures. Faulkner has been consistent in both attitudes. Likewise, there is considerable evidence outside of "Lo!" of a distaste for rigid and impersonal legalisms (which ignore context, human difference, and the counsels of wisdom and experience) such as he ironically expresses in this story. An example is the account of what the people in a rural Missouri hamlet do in defense of the motley trio who "rescued" (i.e., stole) a racing stallion from a life on a brood farm. [56] But nowhere else does Faulkner so quietly or humorously expose the "demon of the absolute." [57] "Lo!," Faulkner's parable of misguided federalism, is the product and the explanation of the combination of a tolerant but warm humanitarianism (which recognizes Faulkner's critics would do well, if they are to read him right, to admit and understand how basic the imperative and the true meaning of brotherhood) and a wise distrust of "democratic dogma" to his perspective upon the world is this combination.

---

56   William Faulkner, *A Fable* (New York: Random House, 1954), 163-189.

57   A phrase presumably borrowed from Paul Elmer More's 1928 volume: *The Demon of the Absolute: New Shelburne Essays*. [Ed.]

3.

Escaping Westward: Faulkner's "Golden Land"[58]

"Golden Land"[59] is one of William Faulkner's neglected stories. It is not part of the Yoknapatawpha cycle; it is not a Southern story, not a tale of post-war disenchantment or of the "folklore of speed."[60] Yet it is a most important story, for it contains Mr. Faulkner's most searching critique of the unnatural and escapist aspects of life in modern America.

The "golden land" is Southern California, and "golden" is here assuredly ironic. But the interest of the story is not in its satiric handling of the tinsel glitter of the Golden West. For it is basically a study of why people come to California, what they come for, and

---

58   This essay was originally published in *The Georgia Review*, Vol 19, No. 1 (Spring 1965), 72-76.

59   *Collected Stories of William Faulkner* (New York: Random House, 1950), 701-726. "Golden Land" first appeared in *The American Mercury* (May 1935), 1-14. [Ed.]

60   This memorable phrase refers to Faulkner's interest, especially in his early work, in the romance of aviation as it emerged during World War 1 and for some years thereafter. The phrase first appeared in a review that he wrote in 1935 of a book called *Test Pilot* by Jimmy Collins. The review was first published in *The American Mercury* (Nov. 1935). Faulkner was somewhat disappointed in *Test Pilot* and wrote: "I had hoped to find a kind of embryo, a still formless forerunner or symptom of a folklore of speed, the high speed of today which I believe stands a good deal nearer to the end of the limits which human beings and material were capable of when man first dug iron …." (389). [Ed.]

what they hope to escape by coming. To Faulkner, as to Robert Penn Warren, the West is a metaphysically significant place to Americans who, though not born in the West, go there compulsively. The principals in "Golden Land," Ira and Samantha Ewing (mother and son), have come to California from Nebraska; but according to Faulkner, the move was not good for them, or for Ira's family. For the Ewings come to California because Ira (the son, now forty-eight as the action of the story begins) wished to "escape" Nebraska and the life his parents had made for themselves there; and Faulkner allows no one to escape. Ira Ewing, Jr. is the hard son of a hard father. His birthplace, a little town on the Nebraska plains, had been founded by and named after the elder Ira Ewing. But young Ira was unable to understand what his father saw in the hamlet he had founded or why he had seen fit to establish it in the "treeless immensity"   of Nebraska. And so at fourteen, though with logic and reason he could not explain why and in the name of what dream of his own he did so, young Ira grabbed the brake-beam of a California-bound freight.

He could not understand his father and mother's talk of "fortitude, the will to endure."[61] Instead, he wanted and got for himself (and for the family he acquired in California) "luxuries and advantages which his own father not only could not have conceived in fact but would have condemned completely in theory."[62] "Golden Land" has to do with the day in Ira Ewing's life when he discovers just what the consequences of his flight from Nebraska have been.

On the surface Faulkner seems to be commenting in this story on the effects of luxury on the character of the Ewings, their fellow Californians, and perhaps on all modern Americans. And this reflection on luxury is certainly part of the burden of the story. The key to Ira Ewing, Jr.'s plan of life is to be found in his intentions to make it "easy" for his family. But the response to his paean on "ease" given to him by his mother, Samantha Ewing—her insistence that things have been too easy for him and his, that the "Lord never

---

61   *Collected Stories*, 712.

62   *Collected Stories*, 703.

intended for it to be" easy for the Ewings[63]—points toward the true theme of "Golden Land"—that suffering, struggle, effort, and "endurance" are necessary to the formation in man of all those traits which give life meaning and dignity.

In the minds of the Ewings (father, mother, and son) the great plains, vast and unchanging, have a significance like that of the big woods to Faulkner's rural Mississippians. The woods, to them, are an objective correlative for that in man's life which is given, *a priori*, "other," for that with which man must come to terms in "pride and humility."[64] Samantha and Ira, Sr. had purposefully defined and measured themselves against the indifference and otherness in Nature and had together (for they became to their son like blood brother and sister, even twins) in their travail "gained a strange peace through fortitude and the will and strength to endure."[65] Faulkner uses the same language to describe them in their relationship to the Nebraska plains that he uses to describe the feeling his initiated hunters and woodsmen have for the "brooding and ineffable" forests in the big bottom.[66] And Ira, Jr., when he at fourteen finds his parents to be "strangers as though of another race," like giants in the shadow they cast—not in size, but in the aura which surrounds them—has an experience parallel to what Faulkner's post-bellum Mississippians feel when they ponder their forefathers, an experience like that of the government agent in "The Tall Men" when he first visits the McCallum clan. In rejecting the discipline of the plains, Ira is like Major de Spain, who, in "The Bear," sells the big bottom to a lumber company and thereby identifies himself with the new commercial and "non-enduring" spirit which will destroy southern society. He is one with Thomas Sutpen in *Absalom, Absalom!* and with all of Faulkner's characters who have a design, a private dream they would impose on the world.

---

63 *Collected Stories*, 724.

64 *Go Down Moses* (New York: Random House, 1942), 233. [The quote is taken from "The Bear."]

65 *Collected Stories*, 712.

66 The Mississippi hunting grounds featured in "The Bear" and elsewhere. [Ed.]

The peace which Faulkner pictures as [belonging to] the elder Ewings, the peace which Samantha wishes to return to and die in at the end of "Golden Land," is expressive of Faulkner's abiding agrarianism.[67] Out of a right relationship to Nature, out of an ability to endure creaturehood and the rest of the human condition in "pride and humility," comes social and moral order. To Faulkner the epitome of man's attempt to escape Nature and his role in it is the city; and in this story Southern California is *the city*, the artificiality of urban life at its most characteristic. And what has happened to Ira Ewing, Jr.'s family (and by implication to all of the decadent glitter of life in the phony, seasonless world of Southern California) is the inevitable consequence of such a flight.

Twenty years before the events in "Golden Land" take place, at the time of the elder Ewing's death, his wife Samantha let herself be moved to California by her son. She agreed to make the move hoping to help Ira, Jr. bring up his two children, Voyd and Samantha (her namesake). She did not intend to "attempt to make another Ira and Samantha Ewing of them; she had made that mistake with her own son and had driven him from home. She was wiser now; she saw now that it was not the repetition of hardship: she would merely take what had been of value in hers and her husband's hard lives—that which they had learned through hardship and endurance of honor and courage and pride—and transmit it to the children without their having to suffer the hardship at all, the travail and the despairs."[68] Samantha, in brief, accepted the fact that she would

---

67   The peace the elder Ewings found in their Nebraska life was fundamentally religious. Faulkner's discussion of it strongly suggests the affinity of his outlook with that of the Nashville Agrarians. In the Introduction to *I'll Take My Stand* (New York: Harper & Brothers 1930) the authors state: "Religion can hardly expect to flourish in an industrial society. Religion is our submission to the general intention of a nature that is fairly inscrutable; it is the sense of our role as creatures within it. But nature industrialized, transformed into cities and artificial habitations, manufactured into commodities, is no longer nature but a highly simplified picture of nature. We receive the illusion of having power over nature, and lose the sense of nature as something mysterious and contingent. The God of nature under these conditions is merely an amiable expression, a superfluity, and the philosophical understanding ordinarily carried in the religious experience is not there for us to have" (xiv).

68   *Collected* Stories, 722-723.

now be dependent because she believed that she could earn her way by passing on the traditional wisdom of the Ewings (for whom "[t]his world has never been easy..."[69]) to her grandchildren. But she is never given a chance. Both her daughter-in-law (as she expected) and her son (to her surprise) encourage, through permissiveness and a desire to make it easy, their children to adopt ideals other than "undeviating incorruptibility" or "honor and dignity and pride."[70] They allow their children to play the thief to life; and they do not make them earn anything or face the consequences of any of their childish misdeeds.

After Ira, Jr. and his wife encourage the children to face down their grandmother when she accuses them (with evidence) of theft, Samantha begins immediately to plan for her return to Nebraska and for her death. But her son will not let her return; though he provides for her amply, he keeps her without money. As part of his general defiance of Nature, he insists on keeping his mother alive, even after he has deprived her of her reason for living. And though he seems to suspect that she wishes to die, he cannot understand why she would any more than he can understand why she and his father liked "that way of living"[71] which they had followed in Nebraska.

Samantha had warned her son fifteen years before the time of the story that this "whole country is too easy for us Ewings."[72] She is forced to see her prophecy come true. Voyd, Ira, Jr.'s son, lives up to his name. At twenty, he is the victim of his parents' permissiveness, and especially of his overprotective mother (who has helped make him homosexual by teaching him to hate and to reject his father). The daughter, Samantha, has under her stage name of April Lalear, become involved in a public sex scandal in her efforts to secure a role in a motion picture production. She is obviously a comment on what happens to beauty when it becomes a commodity. Ira, Jr. is unable to understand why his children have become so ill behaved,

---

69   *Collected Stories*, 724.

70   *Collected Stories*, 723.

71   *Collected Stories*, 720.

72   *Collected Stories*, 724.

"After all I have tried to do for them—."[73] But, we discover, they have merely followed his example. For, once his daughter's sins have been made public and his name linked with hers (at his own expense), he tries to get some cheap advertising advantage for his real estate business out of the scandal. He is no more a natural father than are they natural children.

Moreover, for the past ten years Ira, Jr.'s marriage has been a marriage in name only. He has a separate life with an aging mistress of whose fading appearance he is ashamed.[74] Age, like death and discipline, earning and endurance, can have no place in a world that defies the natural. Everything in Ira's life—his home, children, marriage, business, treatment of his mother, even his joyless drinking (done in assertion of his "youthfulness")—fits the pattern of his rebellion against the limited and contingent status of man in creation, against the necessity of man's earning a place in the face of this status.

But although Ira is willing to make capital out of his family's degradation, at least part of his nature rebels against this. He says to his mother, "you want to run from it. So do I!"[75] And later, when his wife confronts him with a newspaper and blames him for what has happened to their daughter, he replies, "That not the question. That's all done. The question is, what to do about it. My father would have known. He did it once."[76] What his father had done was to put the torch to a rat-infested barn which could not be purged otherwise. However, Ira is not about to take the kind of action his respectful reference to his father's example suggests. He is far too deeply enmeshed in the corruption which he is only beginning to recognize for what it is. And at the story's end, his mother acknowledges the degree of his involvement. She looks out over the land of "golden days unmarred by rain or weather, the changeless beautiful days," a

---

73   *Collected Stories*, 717.

74   *Collected Stories*, 721.

75   *Collected Stories*, 714.

76   *Collected Stories*, 709-710.

land from which Nature itself seems to have been exiled (and hence an appropriate refuge for those in flight from Nature's discipline) and says to herself, "I will stay here and live forever."[77]

"Golden Land" is a story about America in mid-passage, about a family suspended between its homely but substantial agricultural roots and its uncertain urban future. Its conclusion expresses unequivocally William Faulkner's reservations about the motivation, psychology, and morality behind the transformation of the predominantly agricultural society into which he was born into the urban and industrial society to which he addressed himself as a mature artist. And it illuminates by comparison Faulkner's other works which insist that man must endure if he is to prevail.

---

77 *Collected Stories*, 726.

4.

Faulkner and the Jeffersonian Dream: Nationalism in "Two Soldiers" and "Shall Not Perish"[78]

Many of Faulkner's least noted but not least valuable short stories are about the plain people of Yoknapatawpha County, the yeoman farmers of the hill country above Frenchman's Bend. The role of these characters in his novels is usually peripheral; Byron Bunch is one of them, as is the convict in "Old Man."[79] And their archetypes, the McCallums, play a major role in *Sartoris*. His treatment of them is always affirmative and admiring; but in "Two Soldiers" and its sequel "Shall Not Perish,"[80] Faulkner goes beyond admiration to make of one family of plain people, the Griers, the ground for his most openly patriotic statement; and, in the process,

---

78 Originally published in *The Mississippi Quarterly* Vol. 18 (Spring 1965), 94-100.

79 Byron Bunch is a character in Faulkner's *Light in August* (1932). "Old Man" is a novella, first published as part of the interwoven dual narratives in *Wild Palms* (Random House, 1939). [Ed.]

80 "Two Soldiers" was first published in March, 1942 by *The Saturday Evening Post*; "Shall Not Perish" was originally published in *Story* magazine in 1943 as part of an issue devoted to war stories. Both tales are included in *Collected Stories of William Faulkner* (New York: Random House, 1950). [Ed.] Cleanth Books has included an illuminating discussion of Faulkner's yeomen in the second chapter ("The Plain People") of his monumental *William Faulkner: The Yoknapatawpha Country* (New Haven: Yale University Press, 1963), 10-28; it does not, however, refer directly to these stories.

he aligns himself with the age-old Jeffersonian conception of the republic which is still very much alive in the South, though now rarely voiced in such unequivocal terms.

The Griers are a family of small freeholders. They have seventy acres, which their family has lived on and out of for generations. Their mediocre land has supported them because "they had done right by it,"[81] had used it in a spirit of stewardship in (to use one of Faulkner's favorite expressions) "pride and humility." They have asked no man's help and have derived from their freehold and the independence it gives them a sense of self-respect and dignity which, these stories tell us, can outlast the worst of tragedies. Like all [of Faulkner's] pine hill families (the Gowries, MacCallums, Quicks, and Bookwrights), the Griers are clannish and close: like their neighbors they are taciturn, stubborn, and deliberate. Moreover, in their implacable but earned pride, they are willing—like their slaveless yeoman forefathers in whose memory Faulkner remained rather "unreconstructed" in his attitudes toward the War between the States—to shed blood to preserve their independence, and that of their nation, to keep the freehold intact. To them Faulkner turned in these stories to find a reason and a justification for America's role in the Second World War.[82]

"Two Soldiers" is an account of Pete Grier's decision to enlist, of his departure for Memphis, and of how his brother (the unnamed eight-year-old narrator of the story) followed him there. It is simply and directly told. As was noted, the Griers are not talkative; and when they do speak, their language is deceptively simple and archaic. Therefore, the modern reader must infer the implication of Pete's act from the tone Faulkner uses in handling the story—from the action itself and from how that action objectifies his world-view—just what his words and those of his brother and parents mean.

---

81 *Collected Stories*, 102.

82 Faulkner's short story "The Tall Men" was also written during World War II and is likewise about the plain people and their reaction to the war. I have discussed its implications in "Faulkner's 'Tall Men'" [Chap. 1 in the present volume].

As "Two Soldiers" begins, Pete is nineteen; he and his brother go nightly to stand under Old Man Killegrew's window and listen to the war news (the old couple are deaf and play their radio at full volume). When Pete hears of the Japanese attack on Pearl Harbor, he is deeply stirred; as his brother notices, and though he is silent for a few days, he is constantly wrestling with himself. He lies awake nights, rigid in his bed. Then he announces, first to his brother and then to his mother and father, that he must enlist. As he tells the boy, "I got to go ... I jest ain't going to put up with no folks treating the Unity States that way."[83] Pete does not go out of love of battle or boyish vainglory; he is content with his home and loath to grieve his parents. But as one of Faulkner's plain people, he knows that independence and dignity are often to be secured only with blood; and that doing "right by the land" often calls for more than husbandry. In brief he realizes that freedom and the pride it makes possible must be earned and re-earned.

Pete's mother and father react strongly to his announcement and, for a time, try to find arguments to dissuade their son; but they do so out of love for him, not to deny his decision. They understand what obligation it is that he feels, that it is not to some abstract political ideology, but to himself as a free man whose freedom is in question whenever his "land," his country (as he understands it)—the vehicle of his fierce and independent dignity—is under attack. They understand the personal affront Pete feels at Pearl Harbor. Even as the Griers argue that their family has already (for reasons like those their son now offers for his conduct) done service in World War I, they acknowledge their "duty" in this new war. In the end they, send their son away with the solemn, restrained formality which is characteristic of their kind. Their parting words to Pete (words which help to explain what code it is he acts out of in his decision to enlist) are: "Don't never forget who you are. You ain't rich and the rest of the world outside of Frenchman's Bend never heard of you. But your blood is good as any blood anywhere, and

---

83   *Collected Stories*, 83.

don't you never forget it."[84] Pete Grier acts out of, in defense of, the self-respect which his family (and all his people) earned and re-earned repeatedly before he was born, at Kings Mountain and New Orleans, at Shiloh and in Flanders. Their conviction of their own worth requires of them that they not forget who (and how) they are; when a military challenge makes them remember, they shoulder muskets. And in the special and often historically misunderstood spirit of their yeoman freeholder prototypes throughout history, the American, English, and Roman citizen-soldier, they "come to scratch" in fierce unanimity and fight their wars in a particularly personal spirit.

Pete's little brother follows him to Memphis, up Faulkner's favorite highroad to self-discovery. His behavior in his futile attempt to join his brother reinforces the impression of the character of the Griers given us by the first half of "Two Soldiers." Little brother will be (or already is) an intrepid warrior. He tells Pete, "You'll whup the big uns and I'll whup the little uns,"[85] and he offers to cut anyone who would patronize or interfere with him. His trip is proof of his clannishness, his sense of family loyalty and family pride. Once in Memphis and frustrated in his efforts to find Pete, he is as reluctant to accept help and as close-mouthed about his business as any full-grown hill man. His gesture is only a repetition or extension of his elder brother's, and it does not alter the meaning of the story established before he commences his private war against Japan.

"Shall Not Perish" picks up some time after Pete Grier's departure from his family's Mississippi farm. Its occasion is a pair of deaths, that of Pete, and some months after, of the son of Major de Spain. It includes and expands the meaning of the themes already established in "Two Soldiers." Pete's brother is again the narrator; but the protagonist is now his mother. Yet, in this story her "action" (apart from a short physical journey which makes it possible) is not so much a deed as it is talk, a choric commentary of her own values and those

---

84   *Collected Stories*, 87. For a similar injunction by one of the plain people to a son departing, see "The Tall Men," in *Collected Stories*, 53.

85   *Collected Stories*, 83.

of her dead son. And by directing her remarks to Major de Spain at the time of his own son's death (the news of which has driven him to the point of suicide), she converts their common tragedy into an assertion (reinforced by the younger boy's extension of her remarks) of the Jeffersonian ideal of a Republic of "independent" men—and in the process gives to the two boys' death a justification which appears to console de Spain.[86]

Essentially, Mrs. Grier's task in her interview with Major de Spain is to convince him of what her family already knows and understands about their loss and the war, that "there was some point to why we grieved," that the death of the boys has served a meaningful purpose that will make them forever "is," not just "was."[87] De Spain cannot accept his son's death because, as he sees it, his son died for "the folly and rapacity of politicians, for the glory and aggrandizement of organized labor"—in the service of "poltroonery and rapacity and voluntary thralldom."[88] According to De Spain, his son "had no country: ... His country and mine both was ravaged and polluted and destroyed eighty years ago...." Like his forefathers he agrees with Jefferson that there is no value in a society in which "dependence begets subservience and venality, suffocates the germ of virtue and prepares fit tools for the designs of ambition."[89] Mrs. Grier's answer to his argument, the answer which consoles him, and the answer which the very existence of the Griers and people like them supports, is that the old Republic is not dead, that the anthill of contemporary American life is a passing phenomenon, a temporary falling away from "the old verities," that the nation's people are yet "capable of courage and honor and sacrifice," qualities which Faulkner's yeomen act out in their unheralded lives. She admits that "it will take time," but insists "they will learn it" (i.e., will re-learn it—in experiences

---

86 *Collected Stories*, 110-115. Major de Spain is a prominent figure in Yoknapataw-pha, appearing in a number of the novels and short stories.

87 *Collected Stories*, 103-104.

88 *Collected Stories*, 108.

89 Thomas Jefferson, *Notes on the State of Virginia*, ed. William Peden (Chapel Hill: University of North Carolina Press, 1954), 165.

like the war).[90] Wars fought to preserve freedom and "independence" will, she implies, make men more aware of the importance of both to a meaningful life and of the earning, the sweat and blood required of men who should preserve them. This war, she believes, will recall the United States to something of its forsaken destiny; what the two boys have done convinces her that she is right.

Mrs. Grier had foreseen that Pete would die in the war from the time he left home. She does not pretend to understand all that has been intended or accomplished by providence in her son's death. But she does know that what he decided "must be all right, even if I couldn't understand it. Because there is nothing in him that I or his father didn't put there."[91] With this final word she turns to leave; but De Spain, touched by her argument, delays her with a question: "What you and his father gave him. You must know what that was." She answers simply, "I know it came a long way. So it must have been strong to have lasted through all of us. It must have been alright for him to be willing to die for it after that long time and coming that far."[92] Like most country people Mrs. Grier has difficulty in verbalizing the "word" she lives by in any but concrete terms. But it is not difficult to determine from the context in which she makes this answer to De Spain that the "strong" quality which sustained her son in his decision (and her in her sorrow) is the unique republican virtue of which Jefferson believed God had "chosen" to make "his peculiar deposit" in the breasts of "those who [like the Griers] labor in the earth," the yeoman freeholders or those who follow the political and moral tradition they established in the seedtime of the Republic.[93] It is the old virtue come from as far away as the field of Maldon, upon which (in a spirit similar to that of Pete Grier) Byrhtnoth the earl cried to the invading pirates, "Hearken, Vikings, what this folk

_____

90   *Collected Stories*, 108.

91   *Collected Stories*, 109.

92   *Collected Stories*, 110.

93   *Notes on the State of Virginia*, 164-165.

say. We for tribute will give you spears."[94] To this same fierce Anglo-Saxon intrepidity Faulkner attributes the westward development of the nation.[95] This spirit or "blood" (as Mrs. Grier might have called it) is what lived in and through her son and young de Spain, reasserted and preserved itself in their deaths – and was made to seem all the more worth preserving by those deaths.

With this interview the narrative proper in "Shall Not Perish" ends, and the boy-narrator takes off on his own; the results at first appear digressive, out of keeping in a short story. Abruptly, the boy reflects upon his and his mother's visit to the local museum after they have left de Spain's. The museum is a place where people (in a gesture like Pete's) have, as artists, given of themselves "out of love of what they have seen or where they had been born or lived.... "[96] By association, one affirmation leads to thoughts of another; and soon, a third is involved in a further expansion of the implications of young Grier's death.

The trip to the museum recalls to the narrator his grandfather and another trip to town made by the Griers years before Pete's death. The elder Grier had spent his last years in his son's house, buried deep in retrospection upon the War between the States and upon the untainted images of his memory of noble men and deeds. His recollection is not partisan; what he cherishes in memory is neither Southern nor Northern, but is rather the spirit in which both sides fought. From time to time he would start out of his slumber on the porch or under a tree and cry, "Look out! Look out! Here they come!"[97] But his hollering was not, the narrator came to realize, born of fear; when the old man had been awakened by a violent equestrian episode in the Saturday afternoon cowboy feature (to which, as a

94 *Poems in the Old English*, eds. Jackson J. Campbell and James L. Rosier (New York: Harper and Row, 1962), "The Battle of Maldon," 53, ll. 45-46. Byrhtnoth was a Saxon hero who died at the Battle of Maldon in 991 while defending his people against Viking invaders.

95 See *Big Woods: The Hunting Stories of William Faulkner* (New York: Random House, 1955), 4-5.

96 *Collected Stories*, 110.

97 *Collected Stories*, 112.

treat, the Griers had taken him) and had for a moment confused what he saw upon the screen with what he remembered, he rose to his feet and gave the alarm: "Forrest! Forrest! Here he comes! Get out of the way!"[98] After he had scrambled outside and stood blinking and trembling in the sun, his angry and/or amused family followed after him. His son offers reproach to the old man; but Mrs. Grier, in this as in all else, understands her people. She chides her husband and, with the prescience she employs thereafter in interpreting her son's enlistment and death, finds the meaning of her father-in-law's "alarming" habit. She declares, "He wasn't running from anybody! He was running in front of them, hollering at all clods to look out because better men that they were coming, even seventy-five years afterwards, still powerful, still dangerous, still coming!"[99]

In other words, Grandpa Grier's outcries are salutes born of the excitement and uplift of spirit which comes to the hearts of men as they contemplate that which Mrs. Grier says "came a long way" and "was strong to have lasted through all of us" and "all right for him [Pete] to be willing to die for"—the ability of free men to endure, to act, to frustrate all those who would dictate the terms on which they will be allowed to live.

And young Grier, the narrator, concludes "Shall Not Perish" in the spirit of his grandfather's outcries, in exultant tribute to "the men and the women who did the deeds, who lasted and endured and fought the battles and lost them and fought again because they didn't even know they had been whipped, and tamed the wilderness and overpassed the mountains and deserts and died and still went on as the shape of the United States grew and went on ... still powerful and still dangerous and still coming."[100]

With this utterance he usurps his mother's choric role. And perhaps one theme of the two short stories here under discussion is his "education," the completeness of which his replacement of

---

98 *Collected Stories*, 113.

99 *Collected Stories*, 114.

100 *Collected Stories*, 114-115.

his mother gives evidence. I leave this question open. But we can, I believe, be more certain about the thematic implications of these two stories: They are part of Faulkner's intense re-examination of his heritage—the part which attempts to relate that heritage to the Second World War. That he should choose to establish this connection through yeoman characters like the Griers is, I believe, significant evidence of his participation in and identification with one portion of his intellectual inheritance as a Southerner, the Jeffersonian dream of the freeholder's Republic of independent men who will "keep alive [the] sacred fire [of liberty]."[101]

---

101 *Notes on the State of Virginia*, 165.

5.

Faulkner's "Tomorrow" and the Plain People[102]

Faulkner criticism has not thought well of *Knight's Gambit*; and though the collection for the most part deserves the modest estimation it has received, one portion of it, the story "Tomorrow," has suffered unjustified neglect because of the context in which it appeared.

Though it has obvious merit as an independent work of fiction, "Tomorrow" should be approached as a part of Faulkner's admiring study of the plain people of Yoknapatawpha County, in a framework established by such fictions as *As I Lay Dying*, "The Tall Men," "Two Soldiers," "Shall Not Perish," "Race at Morning," and the portraits of Byron Bunch in *Light in August*, the convict in "Old Man," and Mink Snopes in *The Mansion*. The function of the story in the loose framework of *Knight's Gambit* is to explain in part how Gavin Stevens learned his business as county attorney. The events upon which it turns are slight: One of these plain people, an obstinate Frenchman's Bend farmer, for no evident reason hangs the jury in Steven's first case. A justifiable homicide has been committed by a father (one of the Bookwrights) protecting his daughter from the wiles of a flashy seducer, a worthless fellow by the name of Buck Thorpe. But the

---

102 This essay was originally published in *Studies in Short Fiction* Vol. 2, No. 3 (Spring 1965): 235-240.

farmer will not be a party to Bookwright's release. Fortunately, his obstinacy occasions no disaster; for, as we learn subsequently, the vengeful father was exonerated in a second trial. However, in his characteristic manner, Faulkner's most talkative and in some ways most perceptive observer of life in Yoknapatawpha will not let the matter of this first trial rest without an explanation. Gavin Stevens must know why the farmer, one Jackson Fentry, has thwarted justice and rejected his well-reasoned plea to the jury—appealing to the unwritten law, which he would have expected a hill farmer from Frenchman's Bend to understand and accept. And the explanation which Stevens gets is in fact the real story Faulkner intends to tell us in "Tomorrow," a story of human loss and frustration that gives meaning to the protest they provoke.

In attempting to understand the behavior of Fentry (who is the protagonist in this story), it is necessary to remember who and what he is. The Fentrys own a small hill farm (bad land and not enough of it). They eke out a bare living upon it, from generation to generation. But they do *own* their land and keep it and themselves free of debt and clear of other obligations. They endure—"beholden" to no man, taciturn and implacable, until they fall "dead between the plow handles."[103] All they have is their pride; but it is what they and their kind of Yoknapatawpha live on—and Faulkner admires them for it. For such pride as they have, balanced by the humility implicit in their endurance of impossible circumstances and earned by that uncomplaining endurance, is part of what Faulkner believes makes human life worthwhile, gives it dignity.

But to complete the pattern of such a life, to give full meaning to such endurance as the Fentrys', one thing more is needful—hope, or a "tomorrow." And the vehicle of such hope will be family, posterity, a visible token of continuity and promise of fruition. Faulkner understands well what sons mean to a man, to his struggles with the intractable body of the world. And, as he knew, sons are especially important to the land-loving traditional Southerner. Gavin Stevens discovers that Stonewall Jackson Fentry had once had a tomorrow.

---

103 *Collected Stories of William Faulkner* (New York: Random House, 1950), 92.

And his refusal to acquit Bookwright is directly related to its loss. After Judge Frazier dismisses Fentry and the remainder of the jury whose deliberations and will he has frustrated, lawyer Stevens and his nephew, Chick Mallison (the retrospective narrator in "Tomorrow"), set out after him toward the Frenchman's Bend country in the hills southeast of Jefferson. And there, from neighbor and former employer of his weather-beaten little antagonist, Stevens gets the explanation (*i.e.* stories) he seeks. First, Chick and his uncle attempt to go right up to the Fentry place; but they are driven off by the warning shouts and threatened gunfire of the elder Fentry, who insists "you have badgered and harried him enough."[104] However, they have better luck with the Pruitts (whose place adjoins the Fentrys'); for old Mrs. Pruitt tells Stevens that Jackson Fentry had once had a son, a "tomorrow" which had for a time given to his and his father's unremitting and almost fruitless labors the overplus of meaning which comes when love supplements dignity and pride and gives them an object and an afterlife.

Jackson lost his mother early (women are never much in evidence in Faulkner's stories of the plain people); and the boy had begun at the age of three or less to help his father in the field. But when he was "about twenty-five and already looking forty: he left his father with a Negro to help him work the place; and "risking a year or two to earn a little extra money, against the life his grandpa led," he took a "day-wage job"[105] (a variety of labor repugnant to his kind) at the Quick's sawmill. He held the job over two years and then, as suddenly as he had left, came home—with a goat and a baby boy. And, Mrs. Pruitt tells Stevens, "he raised that boy."[106] The Fentrys politely refused her help with the child, the care and solicitude she offered, taking only (and then grudgingly)—out of necessity—a few clothes; they retained the Negro hand until the baby was big enough to be carried into the field; and, like a Fentry, the boy was working in the cotton not long after he began to walk ("you couldn't see the boy at all; you

---

104   *Collected Stories*, 91.

105   *Collected Stories*, 92.

106   *Collected Stories*, 94.

could just see the cotton shaking where he was.")[107] They named him Jackson and Longstreet Fentry because as his "father" put it, "Pa fit under both of them."[108] And, all indications were, he promised well of growing up to be what his name would suggest—an heir to the tradition of the fierce and often barefoot "cavalry" brigades who stood firm in the face of grapeshot at Manassas and made endless forced marches under the command of the original Stonewall—the slaveless men to whom "the war" had been an invasion and whose self-respect had demanded they pull down their muskets and muster at the courthouse to repel the invader. But circumstances intervene and the little boy, for reasons unknown to Mrs. Pruitt, disappears from the Fentry place; his former "father," when asked about him, replies, "What boy?"[109]

Where Jackson Fentry got the boy and how he lost him Stevens learns on his way back to Jefferson. When he and his nephew get to Varner's store at the edge of the hill country, Isham Quick, a witness at the trial, is there awaiting them. He has a story for them, a story which he had remembered when he "heard your [Stevens'] jury was hung."[110] The story is of the little hill man's tenure at his father's sawmill and of the gaunt, pregnant young woman who wandered up to the cabin the Quicks' had built for him (in two years he had gradually assumed responsibility for the mill) and ended his stay there.

The girl's maiden name had been Thorpe; her husband had abandoned her not long after she had announced her pregnancy. And she had been too stubborn to return to her family and brothers, who had opposed her marriage in the first place. Fentry keeps her (almost against her will) alive; like Byron Bunch in *Light in August* (and unlike the convict in "Old Man"), he falls in love with

---

107   *Collected Stories*, 95.

108   *Collected Stories,* 95. [The word "fit" is a Frenchman's Bend colloquialism for "fought." "Pa" refers to Jackson's own father, who apparently fought under both Stonewall Jackson and James Longstreet during the War, ed.]

109   *Collected Stories*, 97.

110   *Collected Stories*, 97.

the girl because she is dependent upon him, and because he takes responsibility for her. Her condition forces upon him, as does Lena Grove's upon Byron, the role of husband. He comes to think of her as his wife; and after the baby is born he persuades her, while she lies upon her deathbed, to go through a ceremonial marriage with him. When she is buried and the cabin put in order, Fentry gets a goat, hires a buggy, and heads home with the baby boy she has given him.

What happened during the next three years Quick did not know (Mrs. Pruitt has already given Stevens this information); but in the summer of the third year after Fentry's departure, a surrey came up to the Quick mill carrying the Thorpe brothers and a deputy; Quick soon learns they intend to have the boy. He insists on going with them but is not given a chance to warn Fentry. They come upon him as he is cutting wood. The struggle is short; "father" and "son" both put up a fight but the boy is carried away. And Fentry, who has feared this moment all along, is bereft of what the sullen girl and the child she left led him to believe in for a time (a future)—with only a memory and the "money" that the Thorpes tried to give him "for his trouble." Jackson walks away into the woods; he will not listen to Quick's kindly talk of taking the Thorpes to law. He had known better than what he hoped, had built his tomorrow upon a lie. But, as we later learn, his submission to the consequences is only apparent.

Jackson recovers and endures; but years after, Quick was present when the one-time father rode thirty miles to see what the Thorpes had made of the boy who had once been his son, Jackson and Longstreet Fentry. From what he saw he turned away sorrowfully. But in memory of the little boy who became Buck Thorpe, and who might have been (would have been) all the name which once had been his implied, he refused to vote Bookwright free. His gesture may be symbolic, a protest against his earlier loss of all his "tomorrows"; but as the lawyer tells his uncomprehending nephew, "... you wouldn't have freed him either. Don't ever forget that. Never."[111]

---

111   *Collected Stories*, 105. The "lawyer" in this passage is Gavin Stevens.

The form of "Tomorrow" is that of an oral tale built upon a synthesis of two other tales which it encapsulates. Its burden is wisdom, the kind of truth which, says Faulkner, is superior to facts—the truth which poets and country people know very well is better communicated and contained in the moving image of an oral narrative than in the dry abstractions of systematic argument and exposition. The wisdom Gavin Stevens acquired in such experiences as this, his first case, [fostered] his development into the proprietary wise man and choric overvoice which he appears to be in much of Faulkner's later fiction. It is the wisdom that comes of understanding the "human heart in conflict with itself,"[112] of understanding "human beings with all the complexity of human passions and feelings and beliefs, in the accepting or rejecting of which we [humans] had no choice, trying to do the best we can with them or despite them."[113] Faulkner's plain people, or as he calls them elsewhere, the tall men, do as well with or despite the human condition as do any other of his characters. What happened to Jackson Fentry was unbearably cruel. It struck him where he was most vulnerable, gave to him and his father a "deep, dynastic wound" of the heart. For the Fentrys, like the McCallums in "The Tall Men" and the Griers in "Shall not Perish,"[114] have their own version of the southern patriarchal dream of family continuity and establishment, a dream of which Faulkner wholeheartedly approves so long as it does not assume grandiose and self-delusive proportions, so long as it is both humble and proud. They are not so fortunate in its execution as are the McCallums; but, as Jackson tells us with his vote,[115] they cannot be overcome by its frustration.

Faulkner's hard-won and hard-headed optimism about the human future, the faith that man will "endure" and thus "prevail" which he voiced in his speech in acceptance of the Nobel Prize, was based upon his discovery of the Jackson Fentrys among the

---

112   *Faulkner at West Point* (New York: Random House, 1964), eds. Joseph L. Fant, III and Robert Ashley, 64.

113   *Knight's Gambit,* 87.

114   *Collected Stories,* 45-61; 101-115.

115   The vote that results in the story's "hung jury."

lowly of the earth. Our awareness of what Buck Thorpe could have been as a Fentry, coupled with our image of what Buck became in fact (by ironically recommencing with Bookwright's daughter the discouraging pattern which had brought him into the world), might have turned "Tomorrow" toward pathos or even tragedy. But its concluding implications (like those of most of Faulkner's stories of the plain people) are heartening and defiant in the face of any and all disappointments. This is what Gavin Stevens, with his eye bright and his voice exultant, is telling his nephew as they return to Jefferson from Varner's store. For the Fentrys of this world, though denied their "tomorrow," will cherish its image in their heart. And therefore, they will not always or forever be denied.

6.

The Winding Horn:
Hunting and the Making of Men in
Faulkner's "Race at Morning"[116]

Professor Clarence C. Gohdes, in his introduction to the first in
a series of reprints of ante-bellum Southern hunting narratives
to be carried in *The Georgia Review*,[117] has done well to commend
to the attention of all students of Southern life and letters the little
understood importance of field sports to life in the Old South. To
the old-time Southerner, regardless of his station in life, and to
those of his descendants who have kept the old ways, hunting was
and is far more than an amusement or source of food. Of course,
it might and often did provide both. Its ardent devotees probably
thought of it in no other terms. But as their practice of it testified,
the sport had for them another dimension, [for it] functioned as a
communal bond, establishing an entrance way, open to all, into the
fellowship of manliness—a discipline appropriate to all who aspired
to "earn" a place of respect in the patriarchal framework. It served
as an instrument of natural democracy, a test and index by which

---

116   This essay was first published in *Papers on English Literature and Language* 1
(Summer 1965), 272-278.

117   Fall, 1964: 255-260.

the members of a society might take each other's measure beneath the aloof but watchful eye of Nature, which made and impartially enforced the rules of their engagement.

The part played by hunting and woodcraft in the upbringing and development of the capable and genuinely mature man is a commonplace theme with Southern writers, past and present. It appears very early in T. B. Thorpe's "Big Bear of Arkansas" (1841) and in the folk tales of Boone and Crockett; it has central importance in some of the best works of such representative modern Southern writers as Caroline Gordon, Andrew Lytle, Marjorie Kinnan Rawlings, Madison Jones, William Humphrey, and Donald Davidson.[118] It plays a lesser but considerable role in the work of many others. But hunting is in the work of no other Southern writer so serious a preoccupation as it is in the fiction of William Faulkner, whose most widely read work, "The Bear," is perhaps the best known American *bildungsroman*—and a hunting story. One version of it has been collected with and linked to his other tales of the chase in an independent volume, *Big Woods*.[119] And one story in that collection, "Race at Morning," is among Faulkner's finest—important not only for its artistry but also for its clear expression of attitudes present but less obvious in the works with which it is collected and others elsewhere in the Yoknapatawpha Cycle.

The protagonist in "Race at Morning" is one of Faulkner's admirable yeomen, a middle-aged and slightly deaf giant of a man, whom we know only as Mr. Ernest. Its subjects are his "education" and that of his foster son (whose name we are not told)—an education in what Mr. Ernest has known and practiced all his life but that he has had no occasion to formulate in his mind and verbalize until he

---

118   Caroline Gordon, "Old Red," in *The Forest of the South* (New York, 1933) and *Aleck Maury, Sportsman* (New York, 1934); Andrew Lytle, "The Mahogany Frame," in *A Novel, Novella and Four Stories* (New York, 1958), *The Velvet Horn* (new York, 1957), and *At the Moon's End* (Indianapolis, 1941); Marjorie Kinnan Rawlings, *The Yearling* (New York, 1938); Madison Jones, *The Forest of the Night* (New York, 1960); William Humphrey, *Home from the Hill* (New York, 1958); Donald Davidson, *The Tall Men* (Boston, 1927) and *The Long Street* (Nashville, 1961).

119   William Faulkner, *Big Woods* (New York, 1955); "Race at Morning" appears on pp. 175-198.

is forced to do so by the events in the story and by the boy's presence and behavior. In fact, the completion of the boy's induction into the fellowship of hunters is the direct cause of the development of his foster father's ethic into a self-conscious worldview. The setting of the story is the big bottom of the hunts in "The Bear" and "The Old People"—a remnant of the great forest of "Lo," the other Indian stories, and the "Court House" section in *Requiem for a Nun*.[120] Mr. Ernest's hunt is not in the literal sense successful; yet it is as fruitful as any hunt reported in the Yoknapatawpha Cycle. For in it the gruff old farmer (a figure reminiscent of the MacCallum boys in *Sartoris*) finds the self-renewal and regeneration he needs for his return to his duty and place outside the woods, back to the remaining fifty weeks of the year during which he is small planter, foster father, good neighbor, and general steward of his place in the community— the self-renewal to which he "earns" the right with his practice of pride and humility in that place. And at the same time, during the hunt and its aftermath, he brings his foster son to the point where the boy can not only follow his example but also participate in the spirit in which he lives and prepare to assume an expanded version of Mr. Ernest's role in the "business of mankind."[121]

The story, which is seen from the perspective of Mr. Ernest's youthful charge, begins in a low key and lingers with obvious relish on circumstantial details of the preparations for the hunt, some minor anticipatory events in the camp, and finally on the heroic chase of the big buck on the last day of that year's sojourn in the bottom. In camp with the old man and the informally adopted waif are some of the central figures from Faulkner's hunting mythology: Uncle Ike McCaslin, Walter Ewell, and Will Legate. Their dialogue over poker sets the stage for the hunt proper, and for Mr. Ernest's conversation with his ward with which the story concludes. Their talk is of education, the subject of all of Faulkner's hunting stories. Walter Ewell and Will Legate censure Mr. Ernest for neglecting to insist that the boy receive his share of formal education. Ironically, the boy's deportment in camp and his judgment of the men who

---

120 *Requiem for a Nun* (New York: Random House, 1951), 3-48.

121 "Race at Morning," 196.

make up the party, along with his conduct and reflections during the hunt, prove beyond a doubt that he is, in his readiness to play the part' of a man, well "educated." He is already willing and able to carry his weight on the hunt or on the farm, live in time, earn his place in the human family, and accept the exactions imposed upon him by circumstances.

From this conversation we are brought directly to the hunt, to a narrative which is perhaps (all questions of meaning aside) Faulkner's most painstaking account of the chase—rivaled only by the story of Ike McCaslin's first kill in "The Old People"[122] and the descriptions of the actual pursuit of Old Ben in "The Bear." We are by this vivid account of his craftsmanship in action convinced of what we should have gathered already about Mr. Ernest: he is a consummate woodsman. Almost by instinct he anticipates where he and his boy will find the buck, foresees that it will get by the hunters on the stand, and, without trailing it on the last leg of its thirty-mile run downriver, accurately predicts where the deer will turn back and at what time it will again reach the area where the chase began. Mr. Ernest is "at home" in the woods, understands, respects, even loves the game he pursues, and shares with it an understanding of the mysterious rules by which all—men and animals—must abide if the hunting is to be meaningful. He proves his skill, tracks down the buck, and then passes up his shot. In him is revealed most plainly the mind of the true hunter—humble before the order of things under which both he and his adversaries test themselves by acting out their own particular natures, proud of his ability to meet those tests. With each enactment of the ritual, men and animals establish again before the world and to their own satisfaction that they have the right to call themselves men or deer or dogs.

For Mr. Ernest the hunt is complete when he has the buck in his sights and brings down his hammers on an empty firing chamber. As he discovers, however, from his foster son's dismay at the "snick, snick" of his empty gun, he has yet a little more to teach the boy (his

---

122 "The Old People" is one of the interconnected stories in *Go Down, Moses* (New York: Random House, 1942). It was first published in *Harper's Magazine* (Sept. 1940).

full partner in all else) before the boy's forest education is complete. Out of absolute loyalty to and respect for Mr. Ernest (the boy calls Ernest "Mister" but does not so refer to most of the other men on the hunt), the boy accepts what he believes to have been an oversight on the part of the older man, a failure to load his gun. The boy assures Mr. Ernest that he will not report to the other hunters what has passed in the forest. Here, after establishing Mr. Ernest's credentials as a hunter and framing the story with the opening discussion of education, Faulkner has the yeoman protagonist speak, to give verbal formulation to the hunter's code acted out in the chase just completed; and in the next morning's post hunt conversation with the boy, Faulkner has Mr. Ernest bring that code to a new fulfillment as he extends its application to the world beyond the bottom. And no sooner. The talk before the hunt, the chase itself, and the boy's misunderstanding of Mr. Ernest's refusal to kill the deer he has tracked down force the hunter to a decision. The connective implications of this sequence are inescapable.

The terminal conversation toward which the rest of the story builds is preceded by the narrator's inner recapitulation of all that he has seen of Mr. Ernest from the time when his mother and father had abandoned him and the old widower had ridden up to the rent house and had said, "Climb up behind," to the moment when he passes up his shot at the deer. The boy comes out of his private meditations, beginning to understand better his foster father:

> All of a sudden I thought about how maybe planting and working and then harvesting oats and cotton and beans and hay wasn't jest something me and Mister Ernest done three hundred and fifty-one days to fill in the time until we could come back hunting again, but it was something we had to do, and do honest and good during the three hundred and fifty-one days, to have the right to come back into the big woods and hunt for the other fourteen; and the fourteen days that old buck run in front of dogs wasn't jest something to fill his time until the three hundred and fifty-one when

he didn't have to, but the running and the risking in front of guns and dogs was something he had to do for fourteen days to have the right not to be bothered for the other three hundred and fifty-one. And so the hunting and the farming wasn't two different things atall—they was jest the other side of each other.[123]

He can now comprehend (in language most reminiscent of the reflections of another of Faulkner's young hunters, Ike McCaslin in "The Bear"), the "pride and humility" required of a man if he is to "belong" in and to the woods—or the world.[124] Courage to overcome the natural fears which belong to the human condition and pleasure in meeting providentially appointed tests (such as the hunt) go into the making of pride; self-definition in terms of creaturehood and acceptance of the terms under which tenure upon man's mortal estate (including land, family, intelligence, and opportunity) is given—these go into the making of humility. The balance of the two is "endurance"; its consequences, stewardship. As the boy says, not "two different things atall ... jest the other side of each other."

When the boy has come this far toward understanding the code of true hunters (which is really the substance of Faulkner's ethic disguised as a specialized idiom), the last stage of his education, his preparation for a useful life under the natural law is substantially complete. All that remains is for him to apply this wisdom to himself. But to do so is, rather, Mr. Ernest's part. Unaware of what has been running through the boy's mind, and troubled by recollections of their earlier exchange over the escape of the buck, the old farmer responds to the boy's declaration, "All we got to do now is put in that next year's crop. Then November won't be no time away at all"—a declaration marking a new stage in the boy's identification

---

123   "Race at Morning," 195.

124   See "Delta Autumn," the penultimate story in *Go Down, Moses*, 354.

with his foster father's mind and not just with Mr. Ernest's will—by announcing: "You ain't going to put in the crop next year. You're going to school."[125]

Mr. Ernest is not with this announcement saying that his foster son should repudiate the education he has completed as a hunter and woodsman. The point made is rather that a formal education will enable the boy to implement the ethic of the forest in a larger sphere, to expand upon the example his "father" set when he rode up to one of his rent houses, found a deserted boy, and said to the child simply, "Climb up behind." Apparently, Mr. Ernest will urge his ward to become another Buck or Buddy McCaslin, hunter and leader, private man and patriarch. Only the foster father would go the McCaslin twins one better and have the boy to help his people not only in their physical distress but also in their moral and intellectual development—help them to learn (as the boy himself has just done) both what is right and "why it's right."[126] To do as well with his place and circumstances as Mr. Ernest, to continue what the older man began when he adopted an abandoned boy, the boy will have to outdo him; for the boy's opportunity is greater. Mr. Ernest tells him, "The farming business and the hunting business ain't enough. You got to belong to the business of mankind."[127] The assertions recall Drusilla Sartoris' distinction (made for the benefit of her stepson, to help him distinguish the true from the false gentleman) between men with private designs upon the world and nobler men whose dream is not "just Sutpen."[128] At this point Mr. Ernest returns to the subject of hunting; in effect he says that the chase is the thing, not the kill. Earned self-respect, not esteem in the eyes of other men or a big side of venison, is the hunter's ultimate reward. As long as the challenge is there, as long as the buck runs in the forest, life is worth living and hunting worth the effort. The boy, once Mr. Ernest

---

125 "Race at Morning," 196.

126 "Race at Morning," 176.

127 "Race at Morning," 196.

128 *The Unvanquished* (New York: Random House, 1938), 256.

has completed his disquisition, accepts it without question; and the story closes on a muted but affirmative note, as the boy goes to fetch the old man a toddy.

What Faulkner has done is to transform and expand the law of the chase into a homely version of the ideals of chivalry and *noblesse oblige*. He has made of their operation in the life of one man, one "family," an occasion for one of his most optimistic statements of his faith in man's ability to "prevail," an answer to the great waste and tragedy in the lives of most of his characters, a foil to the antithetical career of his greatest hunter and greatest disappointment, Isaac McCaslin. And he has implied that hunting can contribute to the development of young men who will "live" these ideals and give to them the widest possible currency and distribution as a self-conscious force. No one could take the sport more seriously.

When we have had further reprints of hunting narratives from Professor Gohdes and have re-examined references to hunting in southern writings published elsewhere, we will perhaps be better able to determine whether and to what extent the meaning which Faulkner attaches to the sport in the lives of genuine men is idiosyncratic. That he knew the world of the hunter intimately and from firsthand experience we cannot question. And it is also well established that in most rural cultures (like those in north Mississippi) hunting is often connected with the admission of boys into the fellowship and world of the adult male. But the implications of these facts we must leave to conjecture. More importantly we can learn personally from hunting in the rural South of our time, from what to this day is the practice of the ordinary Southerner (who, in all likelihood, will not be able to put his experience or what it means to him into words, will not because it is like much else that shapes his life, too axiomatic for discussion), much that would incline us to give credence to what Faulkner has made of this most serious of pastimes. Though a fair-minded man, he was (like most of his fellow Southerners) impatient with fulminations about the inequity of any social or economic arrangement not postulated on the assumption that status must be earned if it is to mean anything to those who have it. If we read his hunting stories discerningly, we will understand why he believed that it is one of the more important tasks of the contemporary South to find, along with what remains among us of the hunter's code, other rituals which will serve a like purpose. For as Mr. Ernest discovers, and as Faulkner tells us repeatedly, a man or a culture is in one sense incomplete without a son, a "tomorrow" to continue his or its work; and a son who has not been made a man is no son at all.

7.

"Spotted Horses" and the Short Cut to Paradise: A Note on the Endurance Theme in Faulkner[129]

William Faulkner frequently chose a comic vehicle for the development of his most serious themes. The "Old Man" sections in *The Wild Palms* and the entirety of *As I Lay Dying* are cases in point. Another is the first chapter of Book IV of *The Hamlet*, the chapter often (and first) printed independently as the short story "Spotted Horses."[130] The implications of this story, whether read as part of *The Hamlet*, as an independent creation, or as an episode in the Snopes trilogy, remain the same. For "Spotted Horses" is part of Faulkner's general and often repeated comment on the most fundamental of human weaknesses, the desire to get something for nothing, to find a short cut to bliss; and it is an important part of his study of the moral and psychological roots of this pervasive escapism and flight from creaturehood.

Our perspective on the enterprises of the ubiquitous Flem Snopes in this story is essentially that of V. K. Ratliff, itinerant sewing machine salesman-philosopher and moral conscience of French-man's Bend. Ratliff is no compulsive reformer; his view of his fellow creatures is not sanguine. Though elsewhere in the Snopes saga he

---

129   This essay was first published in *Louisiana Studies* 4, no. 2 (Winter 1965): 324-331.

130   William Faulkner, *The Hamlet* (New York: Random House, 1940), 275-340.

actively and at times successfully opposes Flem (when he feels he cannot do otherwise), he takes no overt steps to intervene in the sale of wild stock brought back from the southwest by Snopes and the Texas cowboy. He warns everyone against any bargain Flem would offer; but, as he realizes, there is nothing he can do to stop Flem.[131] In fact, once his advice has fallen to the ground, he finds the response of the men of Yoknapatawpha County to Flem's offer of a bargain an unearned advantage, more interesting and instructive than the wily Snopes' instinctive grasp and exploitation of the appeal to these men of such an offer; for he already knew about Flem and was as yet unsure about just how vulnerable to him the community around Frenchman's Bend had become. In reading the story we should follow Ratliff's example and focus on Snopes' "targets."

The ponies which the cowboy sells for Flem are obviously quite wild; and they do not have the look of working stock or farm animals. Mississippi is not their element; and even if tamed, it is doubtful (although some of the men try to convince themselves otherwise) that the ponies could be put to any serious use by the people to whom they are offered. Moreover, in their intractability and fierce energy, they are suggestive of the untamed forces of Nature so prominent in Faulkner's fiction: the floods in "Old Man" and in *As I Lay Dying*; the brooding forests and wild game in the hunting stories; and the fierce hot wind (which represents a variety of natural forces) in *The Wild Palms*. As Faulkner affirms repeatedly, such forces man may come to terms with—even use a little—but not control or "domesticate." Therefore, the only explanation for the success of Flem's horse sale lies in some compulsive quality in man's nature which the cowboy's "sales pitch" taps and commands. The focus in this study is upon that quality.

"Spotted Horses" turns on the cowboy's (Buck Hipps) gift of one of the wild ponies to Eck Snopes; this calculated largesse gets the sale (which was going nowhere fast) under way and establishes the psychological framework in which it is conducted.[132] It suggests to all

---

131 *The Hamlet*, 281-283.

132 *The Hamlet*, 293-294.

those present the "bargain" or "something-for-nothing" implications of the unusual animals here offered for sale. And it leads all or most of them to ignore what they have previously observed of the worthlessness and ferocity of these wild ponies. Faulkner implies that, once Buck (probably acting on Flem's instruction) has set the bidding in motion in this context, the bidders are predictably human when they respond in a trancelike and automatic fashion and buy (for between three and twelve dollars) all but three of the ponies. They behave in this manner because they are intent on having one of the animals, are willing to pay that much and more rather than be deprived of some small share in a "bargain."[133] Although once the sale is over the new owners are immediately aware of the problems they have acquired with the ponies (especially the problem of taking possession of their purchases), they are not fully cured of their dazed and spellbound frame of mind—of what Ratliff calls "the Texas disease"—until their foolishness comes down on them in the form of a stampede, a stampede which injures several and leads the rest on a fruitless nocturnal chase.[134] Only at this point (in accord with the rules of good comedy), as they return chagrined and empty-handed, temporarily purged by the equine saturnalia, are they free of the "humor" Flem's sale had provoked in them.

When questioned about this story in one of his numerous University of Virginia interviews, Faulkner spoke with understanding and even approval of the natural male inclination which made the denizens of Frenchman's Bend vulnerable to Flem's schemes—the tendency to "dream," to reach restlessly above the easy and commonplace, to reshape and remold reality after their heart's desires. As he puts it, "It is a good sign that a man can always be tolled that way, to buy a horse for three dollars."[135] Always an avid horseman, Faulkner knew that in the South and Southwest ownership of a horse and a place in the saddle still give a man a sense of status and importance. This desire to view the world from horseback is rooted in the old chivalric

---

133   *The Hamlet*, 297.

134   *The Hamlet*, 313.

135   Frederick L. Gwynn and Joseph L. Blotner (eds.), *Faulkner in the University* (Charlottesville: University of Virginia Press, 1959), 66.

ideal of the knight or esquire, in the pride which encourages self-respect and individual dignity; when balanced by humility and acceptance of human limitations and by at least a partial recognition of the inescapable realities, the pull of the earth below (a recognition which Faulkner associates with women), the result is healthy, the issue pleasant. But, as he tells us in the aforementioned Virginia interview, in "Spotted Horses" the ponies "symbolized hope, the aspiration of the masculine part of society that is capable of doing, of committing puerile folly for some gewgaw that has drawn him as juxtaposed to the cold practicality of the women whose spokesman Mrs. Littlejohn was when she said, 'Them men!' or 'What fools men are!'"[136] Here the animals represent folly, not the understandable manly delight to be had in looking at the world from horseback; for they are here not brought forward as a means of asserting an earned dignity but are offered as a "bargain"—just as the old Frenchman's place is later (through salting and silence) represented to Ratliff as a special opportunity to get an unearned profit and advantage, to get quick and easy wealth.[137] And, as with Ratliff and his partners in the diggings at the old ruined plantation, the shamefaced humiliation of Flem's gulls carries with it the implications of Faulkner's judgment upon their presumption and eager self-abasement.

William Faulkner believed that life was hard; as demonstrated in the annual hunts in the big bottom in "The Bear" and "Race at Morning," it was meant to give men the opportunity to test and define themselves against circumstances and other men, and against the given, "ramshackle universe [they are] compelled to live in."[138] In *As I Lay Dying* (1930), the choric Vernon Tull ponders (as he reflects on the difficulty of man's lot and considers all the forces that, apart from his own mistakes, conspire against the "cotton and corn"), why it is that the providential arrangement of things sets difficulties in man's way—and then to answer himself, "'Course it does. That's why it's worth anything. If nothing didn't happen and everybody made

---

136 *Faulkner in the University*, 66.

137 This episode appears in *The Hamlet*, chapter 2. [Ed.]

138 Joseph L. Fant and Robert Ashley (eds.), *Faulkner at West Point* (New York: Random House, 1964), 94.

a big crop, do you reckon it would be worth the raising?"[139] Those who accept this challenge instead of whining about the cruelty of the "supernatural joker" who "runs the show" are the enduring. Among their number are Faulkner's matriarchs and his plain folk, the "tall men" in the story of that title—and their kindred, such as the convict in "Old Man," Mr. Ernest in "Race at Morning," and Grandmother Ewing in "Golden Land." They understand what Faulkner told a group of Japanese students: "[I]t's hard believing but disaster seems to be good for people. But if they are successful too long, something dies ... ." They understand that freedom and dignity cannot be preserved unless people who have them "are educated ... through hardship."[140] They realize that life is valuable only on certain terms, valuable only to independent men; therefore, they insist on earning their way, accepting their responsibilities, doing "the best they can" with their situation. They are not subject to the machinations of a Flem Snopes because they are not often governed by those particular impulses which would play them into the hands of a Snopes. In a word, they have "backbone."

For it is fear, or a kind of cowardice, which spawns and furthers events like the fantastic sale in "Spotted Horses"—fear of the human condition itself; and as Faulkner tells us repeatedly, it is this condition and man's attempt to "cope" with it which are his only subjects. In one of his rare extended public statements, the 1951 address to the members of his daughter's graduating class of the University High School in Oxford, the Mississippi novelist warned his contemporaries:

> Our danger is the forces of the world today which are trying to use man's fear to rob him of his individuality, his soul, by trying to reduce him to an unthinking mass by fear and bribery—giving him free food which he has not earned, easy and valueless money which

---

139 *The Sound and the Fury* and *As I Lay Dying* (Modern Library Edition; New York: Random House, 1946), 403.

140 Robert A. Jelliffe (ed.), *Faulkner at Nagano* (Tokyo: Kenkyusha, 1956), 37.

he has not worked for; ... who would reduce man to one obedient mass for their own aggrandizement and power or because they themselves are baffled and afraid, afraid of, or incapable of believing in man's capacity for courage and endurance and sacrifice.[141]

All the temptations to "non-endurance" which batten upon this fear (the huckster with his offer of bargains, the politician with his offer of security in return for pride, the phony glamour of urban life with its promise of "advantages") are as one to Faulkner. Hyatt Waggoner writes of this story that it has one of its integral elements an awareness of man's situation as precarious. Man's pretension and his folly are amusing not so much because he offends against manners and mores and good sense as because he ignores or misconceives his position in nature. Man's societies are always passing away, all of Faulkner's work says, but the truth of his relation to ultimate reality remains constant. When he is ignorant of, or misconceives, these truths, the result is tragic or comic, depending on our mood.[142]

Elsewhere in Faulkner non-endurance, the misconception and violation of man's "position in nature," does have tragic consequences. Though it comes near to bringing tragedy for the Armstid family,[143] the "dream" which deludes Buck Hipps' customers is not so serious or intense as Thomas Sutpen's (*Absalom, Absalom!*); Drusilla Hawk's (*The Unvanquished*); Temple Drake's (*Requiem for a Nun*);

---

141   This address is available only in Faulkner's original manuscript, but has been quoted in part in various places. The interested reader can find most of it at www.open-culture.com ["Never Be Afraid: William Faulkner's Speech to His Daughter's Graduating Class in 1951"]. A substantial part of the address is also included in the documentary *William Faulkner* (Films for the Humanities and Sciences 2006; Produced by Paul Iacono), currently available on YouTube. [Ed.]

142   *William Faulkner: From Jefferson to the World* (Lexington: University of Kentucky Press, 1959), 211.

143   Henry Armstid, who has a minor role in several of Faulkner's tales (including *Light in August*), is plunged into acute mental distress after foolishly buying one of Flem's spotted ponies, using his wife's money to do so. The poverty of the Armstid family is such that the loss of the five dollars squandered on a useless pony is a serious setback for them.

or Ira Ewing, Jr.'s ("Golden Land"). Flem's gulls survive; but they and their neighbors do not learn any lesson. For throughout the Snopes trilogy—both before the "Spotted Horses" episode (in his deals with Jody Varner and with Will Varner himself) and afterward (in his deception of Ratliff, Armstid, and Bookwright; in his acquisition of a public office and then a place in the bank from De Spain; and his securing official "loyalty" from Eula, Gavin Stevens, Will Varner, and Mongomery Ward Snopes)—Flem bargains his way forward, depends upon man's fear, greed, or unwillingness to live with what he or his have done. The pattern described here is repeated; the weakness here discovered is recurrent. Therefore, this story (or chapter) provides, along with amusement, an explanation in miniature of the collapse of the "old order," the order grounded upon the determination of its members to "endure," the ill-recognized subject of *The Hamlet*, *The Town*, and *The Mansion*. As such, it is an excellent illustration of the unity of theme and perspective that binds together the entire Yoknapatawpha Cycle and gives to it authority and impact.[144]

In "Spotted Horses" Ratliff declares, "A fellow can dodge a Snopes if he just starts lively enough."[145] But, as we learn, he has to want to dodge.

---

144   Critics have long recognized (see, for example, Malcom Cowley in his introduction to *The Portable Faulkner* [New York: The Viking Press, 1949], 13-14) that Faulkner's account of post-bellum Yoknapatawpha is a melancholy chronicle of decline; but they have not attributed that decline to a weakening of the will to endure among the children and grandchildren of the unvanquished. Perhaps the oversight has its explanation in the general approval given by most modern intellectuals to the attitudes which make a Snopes possible.

145   *The Hamlet*, 28.

8.

The Gum Tree Scene: Observations on the Structure of "The Bear"[146]

The scene that concludes William Faulkner's novella "The Bear"[146] provides both a summary of and a judgment upon the action preceding it. The theme of "The Bear" is the importance, to individuals and to societies, of their capacity to sustain that balance of "pride and humility" which Faulkner often calls "endurance." The episode in which the protagonist, Isaac McCaslin, comes upon a manic Boon Hogganbeck beneath a great tree full of frightened squirrels dramatizes the consequences for man of the failure to practice the endurance which the total story (as well as the larger unit, *Go Down Moses,* of which it is a part) "recommends." It is the capstone of and the key to a large design. "The Bear" develops toward this resolution by regular and organically related stages, each of which follows from what has immediately preceded it and makes more inevitable the shape which that resolution will assume. Distracted by the pleasure they take in the character of Isaac McCaslin or the merit of his *de post facto* theorizing, some critics have found a stumbling block in the conclusion of the great hunting story. Though eager to extract from the tale some simplistic and sanguine counsel for troubled

---

146   *Go Down, Moses* (New York: Random House, 1942). "The Bear" was originally published earlier in the same year (May 9, 1942) as a short story by *The Saturday Evening Post.* It has, on more than one occasion, been published as a stand-alone short novel, or novella.

times, they sense in its ending something other than a promise of easy hope. And they should. For, like the interior monologue of Ike (sixty-plus years after) which closes its sequel, "Delta Autumn," the last two pages of "The Bear"[147] imply an ominous future for any who would approach Nature as Boon does when Ike finds him seated beneath that tree; and, again like that monologue, these pages indicate that no other future can be expected, given the impious spirit which Faulkner believes has possessed our age.

In order to reconstruct the framework which makes fully intelligible this grotesque tableau of the maddened woodsman, his broken gun, and the lone tree full of game in whose shadow he raves, we must look back to section four of the novella, to the exchange in the plantation commissary between young McCaslin and his cousin *cum* father, McCaslin Edmonds, in which Ike tells his kinsman what he has learned about man's proper relationship to Nature from his training and experience in the forest—from Sam, Old Ben, the other elder woodsmen and the wilderness itself.[148] Ike finds in the hunt, in the true hunter's reverent approach to the game he pursues and sometimes kills—and especially in the mutual testing, measuring, and self-renewal which the big bear and the men who keep annual rendezvous with him share—a parable, a miniature of the pre-ordained and providentially intended role of man as steward of a creation and a particular place in creation with which he must "cope," though (articulating in his statement the assumptions underlying the pattern of history teleologically interpreted, in Faulker's Yoknapatawpha Cycle), "He [God] created man to be His overseer on the earth ... not to hold for himself ... ."[149] For the hunters the game in the forest, and especially Old Ben, are counters for the "brooding" and numinous presence in Nature, the Arbiter and "Umpire"[150] whom, like the mystery of the land itself,

---

147 *Go Down, Moses,* 330-331.

148 Sam Fathers is a part-Indian tracker who has shared his hunting expertise with Ike; "Old Ben" is the legendary bear that Ike and his cohort of hunters have pursued for years. [Ed.]

149 *Go Down Moses,* 257.

150 *Go Down, Moses,* 181.

man must have the courage to face and the humility to acknowledge if he is to achieve genuine self-knowledge. He must "endure" his position in relation to this ill-defined but transcendent presence if he is to "cope" with his contingent status in a universe arbitrarily arranged to suit something other than his convenience, endure and prevail over his condition. The alternatives are passivity (fatalism) and aggression (Promethean self-assertion), either humility or pride alone. Ike takes the former of these disastrous courses; he ignores the necessary connection of stewardship or the holding of place, property, and position in "fee simple—for God—and power over what is held. But from Boon's words and actions in the Gum Tree Scene, we can infer that he, like the leaders of his culture, has chosen the latter.

But if Ike's long dialogue with Cass[151] explains much about the significance of the final pages of "The Bear," an examination of the fictional order or total sequence of episodes of which these pages are a climacteric tells even more. Sections one, two, and three of the novella are, so far as structure is concerned, a unit. They form together the double story of the last years of Old Ben and the concomitant emergence of Isaac McCaslin, the last of his line, as a man and hunter. The one undercuts the other. The enveloping action of historical change and cultural decline or disorientation represented by the passing of the wilderness and its presiding spirit sets in sharp relief and gives poignance to Ike's inheritance of the mantle of Sam Fathers—of his priestly place as spokesman of the old order. The spirit of reverence, the courage to accept and endure the human condition according to the terms of the God-given covenant, is lost by most of his elders just as Ike begins to understand and share in that spirit. And even he is unable or unwilling to transfer it from the shelter of the hunting camp to the arena of the great world outside the big bottom. Section four gives us not only a philosophical explanation of the elusive elegiac implications of the death of a single bear but also an insight into why Ike will hereafter in the McCaslin

---

151 Cass' birth name is McCaslin Edmonds; he is named after his great-grandfather, "Old Carothers" McCaslin. Sixteen years older than his cousin Ike, Cass assumes a paternal role toward his cousin after Ike's father dies in 1879.

saga serve only as gloss on and chorus to the further progression of the *zeitgeist* toward an apocalypse which he deplores. Ike, like Sam, might have served as at least a stay against such confusion. As "The McCaslin," the patriarch, he would have been of great use to all the inhabitants of his world who had need of a man of his humanity; he might even have forestalled the return of his family's history (in "Delta Autumn") to the very infamy which made him want to stand aside. But once we have witnessed his refusal to "endure" history and his resignation from it in search of an impotent "freedom" and purity, we are prepared to see the shadows deepen,[152] to see the public and general triumph of the forces whose advent had made it time for Ben to die. In section five the darkness falls; the enveloping action finally encapsulates and negates the lonely hunter and the hopeful narrative of his "education"—though even here, perhaps to clarify in unmistakable terms the full burden of the Gum Tree episode, Faulkner reaffirms the freedom of the protagonist from the self-assertive implications of the non-enduring spirit.

The structure of section five itself reflects the design of the entire novella. It moves from a reconsideration and recapitulation of Isaac McCaslin's "progress" toward perfect fellowship with a given and inscrutable natural order to a qualification of the hopeful suggestions of this communion and from thence to a total denial of them. And in the ordering of its contents and the straightforward juxtaposition in that order of materials or themes already developed earlier in the novella, it offers in dramatic terms the plainest possible indication of the entire fable's burden. Section five begins with the announcement: "He [Ike] went back to the camp one more time... ."[153] After adverting briefly to a conversation of young McCaslin with Major de Spain, in which the former makes arrangements for his trip, and after assuring us that the death of Ben did mean the end of an era, that the trip will be valedictory, the narrative moves swiftly to depict the journey itself. Boon, who will join Ike at the camp (as arranged by De Spain), is now serving the lumbering company as marshal of Hoke, the railhead of the company's short line where Ike

---

152 *Go Down, Moses*, 299-300.

153 *Go Down, Moses*, 315.

will leave his horse. His new employment, like the earlier assurances that the doom hanging over the forest sanctuary of the old balanced code will not be revoked, further prepares us for the section's (and the story's) conclusion. But Boon does not meet Ike at Hoke, or even at the place where the wagon road to the old camp meets the tracks. Instead Ash, the camp cook and Negro handyman, picks him up. As he leaves the train, Ike is troubled with the new meaning the "diminutive locomotive" and its incursion into the wilderness has taken on for him. He reflects on earlier trips he has made on it and observes, "It had been harmless then." Now it puts him in mind of "the lingering effluvium of ... death" or a "snake."[154]When Ike gets into the wagon, Ash tells him that Boon is in the woods and expects to meet him at the gum tree. With this announcement the last thread is spun out and we are ready for the denouement. The young huntsman moves up into the woods toward the grave of Sam Fathers and falls into a recollective reverie. The stage is set.

As he muses, the memory of Faulkner's protagonist takes him back to the day when he slew his first deer, and especially to Ash's reaction to his success. Like the hound in section three of the novella, the little bitch who had to go in on Old Ben just once to prove herself a dog, Ash is provoked by the action of another to reach out after the token of his right to a place among his own kind which a part in the hunt would give to him. There is nothing particularly "racial" about his dilemma. His place in the camp is and has been what his role there has earned for him. Sam Fathers, who outside of the woods has little more social status than Ash, is the peer or even (at least in an unofficial way) patriarchal chieftain of the white hunters in the camp. And Ash is normally too down-to-earth to be interested in pitting his energies, much less his life, against wild creatures for which he has no need. But, as the shells he saved over the years make evident, he has felt the impulse to participate in the ritual at least once. After Ash sulks and refuses to cook, he is indulged; but the results of his hunt are abortive. No deer are taken; and on the way back to camp he loses his ancient, unmatched cartridges firing at a little bear he finds in his path. Ike recalls the old Negro, whose

---

154   *Go Down, Moses*, 320, 321, 318.

self-respect has been threatened by the manly accomplishments of a boy, searching in the cane near the spot where he misfired. His impotence as a huntsman, coupled with his attachment to the useless old shells (which in possession he converts into a pathetic prop for his pride—a means of asserting that he could hunt if he so wished, act if he so willed) make of Ash as young Ike remembers him a burlesque and foil to what the boy will shortly behold. With Ash and his impotent weapon, his fat little bear, and his fumbling rage, we edge still closer to the apogean moment.

Ike's reverie moves from past to present from thoughts of the old Negro's pathos to pious tributes to the inscrutable order of Nature, as he realizes he has reached, not the gum tree, but the knoll where Sam and the great dog, Lion, lie at rest. The memory of Ash on the hunt and the Gum Tree scene, in one sense, frame the moment at the grave.[155] This is not to say that the series of three parts is not a progression. Ash's comic gesture of pride and Ike's recommitment to the species of endurance which enables him to celebrate in the cycle of seasons his own finitude—a humility which, he again makes clear, is not in his nature balanced with pride in responsibilities—begins the rapid narrowing of focus upon and specific dramatization of the disintegration of a moral order. This narrowing and concretizing concludes only when we come to the scene beneath the tree. It is most natural that Ike should think of the discipline he acquired there as he moves again through the woods, that he should think of Ash's relation to that discipline as he leaves him to enter the woods, and that he should give us his most lyric and impressive expression of the "understanding" of the human condition with which that discipline has endowed him as he reaches the "temple" of his faith, the burial ground. And nothing could make plainer that the final episode of section and story marks the victory of a vision not at all like that of the protagonist than does the placement of this episode immediately after Ike's moving restatement of his position. But the dynamic of section five (like that of the entire novella and indeed of all of *Go Down, Moses*) is not simply linear. Lines of force run back and forth, zigzag, throughout the story as they move it forward. By

---

155 *Go Down*, Moses, 326-330.

setting between the parody of endurance and the tableau of violent non-endurance the boy's tribute to his spiritual birthplace and to the ordered immortal sequence, the "deathless and immemorial phases of the mother"[156] which he has learned there to accept—and by including in the vista of woods, graves, and mutilated paw above which he accepts in that affirmation the new totem of the wilderness, the snake—Faulkner draws in and ties together the threads he has run out. He thereby makes the Gum Tree Scene a thematic as well as dramatic climax of the novella and not of just its fifth section. The juxtaposition of these details in this particular three-part pattern at the end of this particular five-section sequence should convince us that, for the time, non-endurance has won out, that something more than Ben died in and with Ben, that the numen which once wore the visage of the bear or the many-pointed stag now wears the aspect of the serpent who, as Allen Tate writes, "counts us all."

Isaac's salute to the huge rattlesnake which guards the graveyard knoll immediately precedes the Gum Tree Scene. His very words ("Chief ... "Grandfather") are affirmations of allegiance both to Sam's legacy and to the authority Sam served. They complete his identification with the old Indian's spirit of coexistence with Nature which Sam had cultivated in him. The Indians of the old South had a "traditional reverence for rattlesnakes." Their "Umpire" or "Arbiter," like the one to which Faulkner and his characters often refer, took on various forms (depending upon the role to be played in an encounter with man) an eagle in council, a great bear to young men in search of their manhood, a stag in the hunt for meat, corn to the farmer—and seems to be in character as a snake now when scourging or death is in the offing. As Sam had earlier accepted the necessity of Ben's death, Ike accepts the snake; and with it he accepts (and moves us to accept) the justice of a more concrete and yet elusive trope which follows. The lifted hand and the honorific words in the old tongue tell us plainly that the Fall has been re-enacted in this garden. Natural providence, God, or the Great Spirit (it is unwise to be too specific about the name) has now appropriately punitive implications which are hopeful only in so far as they bespeak an ultimate justice which

---

156   *Go Down, Moses*, 326.

is potentially redemptive by being punitive. Here and elsewhere Ike places his hopes for the future of his people with this justice. But this discussion takes us beyond "The Bear" to the stories which stand immediately after it in *Go Down, Moses*. Only the severity of the judgment of the Gum Tree Scene can therefore give occasion for comfort.

It is particularly appropriate that Faulkner uses Boon in the dark conclusion of "The Bear." For Boon is an unselfconscious victim of the spread of the virus of non-endurance around him, a spread made possible in part by the dereliction of his society's natural leadership; and Boon had once been given a place of the highest honor as the instrumental cause of Old Ben's assumption, a place which could have belonged to him only as one who was totally free of the new presumption. Boon's performance under the gum tree indicates how far and how rapidly the toxin has spread.

As to the final scene itself, we have been reminded throughout section five that Ike will eventually meet Boon in the woods. But the spectacle of his fury and his snarl at his young friend, especially as it comes hard after the religious calm of the scene on the knoll, is nevertheless surprising. The total rhythm of the section gives to the ultimate moment all possible impact and purchase upon our imagination. But its intensity, however well prefaced, would be unendurable if prolonged. Ike's attention is called to Boon by the noise the giant woodsman is making while smashing the barrel of his shattered gun upon its stock. His hysteria is of frustration born. The gun was for him (in his new connection as the co-worker of the locomotive and the lumber mill) a means of establishing a dominion over Nature, represented in all her beauty by the squirrel-filled tree above him. The association of guns and other mechanical devices with the prideful attempt to dominate or "own" Nature was established much earlier in "The Bear" when Ike had his first face-to-face encounter with Ben.[157] That Boon has, like his Indian forefathers, learned from his more "civilized" associates to desire full and single possession of Nature as a sanction for his pride we are

---

157   *Go Down, Moses*, 208-209.

assured by what he says to Ike as the boy approaches: "Don't touch them. They're mine!" Though his impotence with a gun is proverbial throughout the novella, Boon had earlier shared with the regulars in the hunting camp a sense of decorum which made possible their fellowship with one another and, together, with the great bear. But the "greeting" he here gives to a member of that company is proof that he is now of another fellowship; from the immediate context in which his words appear we can determine that he has become a part (and type) of the presumptuous and cowardly attempt to escape creaturehood, the attempt which leads the "new" men to abuse the land, to "gnaw at the flanks" of the wilderness in fear of what it suggests to them about their importance and place in an ultimately mysterious order.[158] What has happened to him at the end of "The Bear" is what an older Ike (perhaps thinking back to this moment) foresees in "Delta Autumn" will happen to all who would cancel their tenure upon the land in and with a spirit of self-aggrandizement, who would acquire an artificial sense of importance at the expense of what they were given in trust. Their success will be their scourge, a Sisyphean torment appropriately created by their wrongful use of the gifts of God and followed by a discovery that these gifts have (because of their crime) become at once theirs and not theirs. As Ike puts it, "The people who have destroyed it [the land] will accomplish its revenge."[159] Ike believes it must be so because God has discovered of His creations that "apparently they can learn nothing save when underlined in blood."[160] Human attempts having failed to halt the spread of the non-enduring spirit (which the first four sections of the story affirm), providence will have to restore the old order of pride and humility from without. With that note, looking forward to a more general punishment and backward to the end of an "enduring" prelapsarian time, "The Bear" concludes.

Some years ago, Robert Penn Warren remarked that Faulkner's fiction presented American criticism with its greatest contemporary challenge. And although in the intervening years the response to his

---

158   *Go Down, Moses*, 193.

159   *Go Down, Moses*, 364.

160   *Go, Down,* Moses, 286.

call has been voluminous, Warren's statement still holds true for today. Since the Nobel Prize Address (in which the contemporary world heard a note of reassurance which gladdened its heart, and then almost at once tried to translate that note into the idiom of its own obsessive political and technological eschatology), Faulkner's critics have devoted themselves to the search for his "message." In the meantime, many have failed to consider the simple but carefully weighted words with which he repeatedly reaffirmed his very old-fashioned patriarchal world-view, words like "pride," "humility," "cope," and "endure." In examining the puzzling design of some of his most important fictions, they have forgotten what Conrad Aiken recognized long ago: that it is Faulkner's characteristic practice to "withhold his meaning," to move from a guarded to a more open exposition of his themes to endow them with the greatest possible authority. That Aiken's observation is correct can be proved out of *The Sound and the Fury, Absalom, Absalom!, Intruder in the Dust, The Unvanquished, Requiem for a Nun*, and many of the short stories. The attempt has here been made to demonstrate that it applies equally well to the unfolding structure of "The Bear." Once the centrality of the endurance theme to the corpus of Faulkner's achievement is recognized, the structural similarity and integrity of most of his work and the dimensions of his commentary upon his times will be much more apparent.

9.

All the Daughters of Eve: "Was" and the Unity of *Go Down, Moses*[161]

The themes which make a unified book of *Go Down, Moses* are (most of them) established in the story with which that collection begins. All are closely related; all reflect upon the dilemma imposed upon man by his obligation to "endure" a difficult but providentially given arrangement of things, to "cope" with the intransigent complexities of the human situation which baffle and inspire him to dream of "freedoms" lost to him and his even before the Fall. And most important among those things which are to be endured are land, women, and the basic social arrangements which the two together compel men to sustain. I refer here specifically to men's endurance (or failure to endure) because, though women exert a constant and sometimes even controlling pressure on male conduct in *Go Down, Moses* (in the title story, in "The Fire and the Hearth," in "Pantaloon in Black," and in the flashbacks of Part IV of "The Bear"), it is upon the choices made by males and upon men's understanding of their proper role that this suite of stories focuses.

---

161   Originally published in *Arlington Quarterly* (Autumn 1967), 28-37.

This first story "Was" has been generally abused and misunderstood by most of the little criticism is has received.[162] All too often it has been assumed that its subject is black slavery and its human cost. Olga W. Vickery sees in it a parody of slave chases commonplace in abolitionist propaganda, an inverted "flight across the ice."[163] It has also been variously described as shallow high jinks, an apologia for the peculiar institution, "horrifying," and a denial of the "moral problem of slavery."[164] However, though "Was" does treat of the involvement of black and white McCaslins, its focus is not upon this relationship. Action antecedent to the story's time established this connection once and for all in the lifetime of the founder of this branch of the family and of their plantation, Old Carothers McCaslin. And to this relation subsequent sections of the book return. Carothers' boys, the lovable bachelor twins Amodeus and Theophilus (who are the story's protagonists), are not concerned with the loss of a Negro; their father left to them more than they know what to do with.[165] Like Frank Meriwether in John Pendleton Kennedy's *Swallow Barn* (1832), they are what Cleanth Brooks has called "singularly undoctrinaire abolitionists," interested in getting rid of slaves, not in acquiring them.[166] It is difficult to say who owns whom on the

---

162　"Was" appears on pp. 3-30 of the Random House first edition of *Go Down, Moses* (New York, 1942). We have had intelligent discussions of this story from John Lewis Longley, Jr. (*The Tragic Mask: A Study of Faulkner's Heroes* [Chapel Hill, 1963], 105-110); from Lawrance Thompson (*William Faulkner: An Introduction and Interpretation* [New York, 1963], 81-85); and particularly from Cleanth Brooks (*William Faulkner: The Yoknapatawpha Country* [New Haven, 1963], 244-248).

163　Olga W. Vickery, *The Novels of William Faulkner* (Baton Rouge, 1959), 126.

164　The most wrongheaded comments on "Was" known to this writer appear in Walter F. Taylor's "Let My People Go: The White Man's Heritage in *Go Down, Moses,*" *South Atlantic Quarterly*, LVIII (1959), 20-32, and in Edmund L. Volpe's astonishing *A Reader's Guide to William Faulkner* (New York, 1964), 232-234.

165　It is recorded that only once did the McCaslins buy a slave, one Percival Brownlee. They purchased from the fabled Nathan Bedford Forrest this negro who was supposedly very "handy" in everything. However, he proves to be their "spotted horse." The painful results of this purchase (considerable financial loss, waste of time, disruption of plantation routine—and another mouth to feed after the worthless slave refuses freedom) do nothing to encourage Buck and Buddy to be sanguine about the advantages of slave holding (*Go Down, Moses*, 263-265).

166　*The Yoknapatawpha Country*, 248.

McCaslin plantation. To the twins their Negroes are a responsibility, not ready for freedom (they free those who are—if they are willing to leave) but not to be selfishly used to serve private designs or
schemes for self-aggrandizement. Their attitude toward their slaves
is the corollary of their use of the land they own, a matter of stewardship, a question of patriarchal tenure for the common good.[167] But
they do not want their mulatto half-brother visiting his girl on the
Beauchamp plantation. And their reasons have nothing to do with
slavery. For Warwick[168] poses a threat to their way of life far more
serious than the most unruly Negro—the threat of a marriage which
could 1(and would) involve them more deeply in the abusive poten-
tial of the plantation system than any innocent attempt to avoid such
involvement. They cannot perceive the necessity of that involvement
for the plan they have undertaken of social and economic reforma-
tion for their own community.

Miss Sophonsiba ("Sibbey") Beauchamp, the source of this
threat, is a comic figure, a middle-aged virgin with a roan tooth and
somewhat ludicrous airs. But she has one thing in common with most
of Faulkner's respectable women, a quality which makes Buck and
Buddy take her quite seriously. She is anxious to get (and manipulate)
a husband. And as Buck and Buddy realize, life on their plantation
cannot continue as they would have it if one of them accommodates
her. Sophonsiba is not comic to the twins; she knows how to use the
"rules" and the forces on her side—"rules" and forces whose general
power or validity the McCaslin boys, as their conduct as hunters,
poker players, and gentleman callers makes plain, never deny. The
inverted version of the stock *amour courtois* pattern (something
which Faulkner, after Bernard Shaw, sometimes suggests that men
invented in their delusion and women keep up in their practicality),
forced on the puzzled Buck while he is at Warwick, suggests that this
"lady," just like most of her "sisters," is a formidable creature.

---

167 *The Unvanquished* (New York, 1938), 52-37.

168 The Beauchamp plantation is called "Warwick" at Sophonisba's insistence because she believes that her brother Hubert is the rightful earl of Warwick, seat of the
ancient English Beauchamps.[Ed.]

Miss Sophonsiba cannot endanger Buck and Buddy unless one or both are at Warwick or she at their place. And they are never at her home but for one reason—to fetch home Tomey's Turl. They (or rather, Buck—Buddy never leaves the McCaslin place unless there is an emergency) have to fetch him home—formally—or face a prolonged visit from their neighbors; hence all the ritual of the hunt. Turl's "visits" across the country line usually come about twice a year. They are part of a calculated strategy on the young Negro's part. He is, by his own admission, in league with women and the earth, with the elemental forces of nature which he knows to be irresistible; indeed, there is even some suggestion that the compact has been formalized in conversation with Miss Sibbey. He doesn't push his elder kinsmen. He runs off frequently enough to keep the pressure on, and no more. But he wants Tennie Beauchamp for his wife. And he expects the McCaslin twins' fear of the way her owners persist in taking their visits to Warwick (not as attempts to retrieve a Negro but as "courtly" calls upon Miss Sibbey) to force them into purchasing Tennie. Turl (or Terrel), like another of Faulkner's wise men, old Ephraim in *Intruder in the Dust*, knows what world he is living in.[169] Buck and Buddy, two idealists, mustarn the hard way.

The trek to Warwick described in "Was" is climactic. In the story of the "hunts" which have been going on simultaneously (Turl's for a wife, the McCaslins' for a restraint on the mulatto boy, Hubert Beauchamp's for a brother-in-law, Sophonsiba's for a husband) are resolved—or almost resolved. With it Turl's design is accomplished, and Miss Sophonsiba's is put well on its way toward completion—even though Uncle Buddy's fabled skill at poker postpones its ultimate fruition for a while. In brief, by prolonging Uncle Buck's stay at the Beauchamp Plantation until darkness falls, Turl arranges an opportunity for the old man's innocence to betray him into a compromising situation. He anticipates that it will be one thing

---

169 *Intruder in the Dust* (New York: Random House, 1948), 112. Ephraim's words (addressed to another young gentleman of learning, Chick Mallison) are: "If you got something outside the common run that's got to be done and can't wait, don't waste your time on the menfolks; they works on what your uncle [Gavin Stevens] calls the rules and the cases. Get the women and the children at it; they works on the circum- stances."

if not another (a word, a look, or a gesture) that will trip Buck up and make him want to be certain that he will not have to visit Warwick again. And the Beauchamps help all they can. Exhausted from pursuing his runaway kinsman, the "woman weak" member of this droll tandem and his nine-year-old nephew (McCaslin Edmonds) wander into a darkened plantation house (an action itself symbolic of Buck's condition in the designing clutches of his hosts) and stumble into Miss Sophonsiba's bedroom. Cass, though more wary than Buck (and forewarned by both Turl and Buddy), is too young to be on his guard against this snare. As the story indicates, he knows nothing of women. There is more than a little suggestion here of a trap (conscious or unconscious). With a guest on the place, the Beauchamps should not have put out all the lights and gone to bed before the McCaslins returned to the house. Miss Sophonsiba's door is left unlocked; she is not asleep (at least not snoring—and we are told that she does snore); and she says nothing when man and boy enter her room—until Buck gets into bed. Once, on a visit to the McCaslin plantation, Mr. Hubert tried to compromise his sister (with her apparent approval) by leaving her under the McCaslin roof. With Theophilus caught, sans trousers, Hubert of course demands that his neighbor do the honorable thing. Buck panics, tries to get out of his troubles with cards, loses his freedom again (and a dowry), and Cass goes for Buddy. The calmer twin for the time being (since he is dealing only with Hubert—another man) manages to extricate his brother from what Beauchamp calls "bear country." For no man can beat Buddy at *his* game. But though the master of Warwick loses at poker (in a handover which Turl "presides" as dealer), in the long run he is a winner. The McCaslins acquire Tennie—and something of a broken spirit. The fulfillment of the prophecy made by Tomey's Turl to young Cass, that women get what they want (at least in such matters), foreshadows Buck's ultimate surrender. This narrow escape from matrimony leaves the twins with much less will to resist the inevitable Miss Sophonsiba. Later on in "The Bear" we learn of her marriage to Buck. She is to become the mother of the central character of *Go Down, Moses*, Isaac McCaslin, in whose recollection this story lives.

Andrew Lytle has called our attention to the fact that women in Faulkner's fiction are the instruments and preservers of community. And for the male, community means compromise. At times Faulkner seems almost to agree with Hawthorne that man's involvement with womankind is a *felix culpa*, at once death to these private and/or idealistic dreams and innocent freedoms and a wisdom-bringing adjustment to "the body of the world." All human relationships have, in proportion to their strength, a delimiting effect on those whom they involve—particularly that of a man to a woman. Because insofar as women represent community and its basic units, family and clan, they establish an order of priorities in a man's obligations to his fellows, an order which may set him at odds with either his own plan for life or with those to whom he might otherwise be well disposed. The interests which women represent are particular, not general. And necessarily so. The species and civilization depend upon the power of the maternal drive to command men's loyalties to what Edmund Burke calls their "own little platoon."

Buck and Buddy are forced by Buck's marriage to Miss Sophonsiba to violate their personal code of ethics and to end their prolonged adolescent (and adolescent it is, however worthy) idyll. They finish the big house (their slave quarters) and become somewhat more conventional planters. To some it might seem that, in the process of responding to their changed status after Buck's marriage, they have put the survival or need of family (and especially the continuation of a family dynasty) above common humanity. But perhaps the point of "Was," and one of the principal themes of *Go Down, Moses* (and the lesson which Cass Edmonds must have learned in the story), is that the value of any man's virtue is slight unless it has an afterlife among his descendants. And descendants may require him to compromise virtue, probably not as much as Miss Sophonsiba would have the twins to, but at least a little—at least as much as Cass does in continuing Buck and Buddy's work and by preparing Ike to continue it after him.

As Faulkner reiterates over and again (in *The Wild Palms*, in the Jack Houston story in *The Hamlet*, in the lives of Joe Christmas and Byron Bunch in *Light in August*, and in the experience of

Ike McCaslin with his wife recorded in Part IV of "The Bear") the consequences of trying too hard to escape from that natural human condition of "fate" which includes women may be worse than that fate itself. Grand and well-meaning schemes and understandable fears notwithstanding, nature will eventually either have its way or exact its price. Community makes possible the continuance among men of the human values which Buck and Buddy affirm—and depends upon the partial violations of those values which women occasion for its persistence. This is the point of the story with which this complex book begins, a point which, as Brooks writes, provides "perspective in which we shall have to view ... Ike's act of renunciation [in 'The Bear']."[170] Here already we are informed that idealism must be tempered by realism, that there is a complexity to true endurance which righteously simplistic readings of "The Bear" (and through it, of the rest of *Go Down, Moses*) ignore. The irony is that the story survives (from Cass) only with the very McCaslin whose life is an attempt to deny its point.

In "Was" we get considerable intimation of what we are told in detail elsewhere in the Yoknapatawpha Cycle, that Amodeus and Theophilus McCaslin are exemplary characters, a little roughhewn and plain-spoken, but as solid as the timbers in their bachelor cabin. They hunt, play cards, "hurrah" each other, try to run their place well enough to feed their people; and on the side lend a hand to their poor-white neighbors. They are Huck and Jim both. Their raft is their plantation. Before this story begins, they have already resolved their problems of conscience vis-a-vis all their Nigger Jims. But their raft too must put into shore and their full manhood begin. Buck has escaped to the territory on more than his share of occasions. And what he has wrongfully escaped is not particularly Miss Sophonsiba but rather what she stands for. The lady of Warwick is perhaps his

---

170   *The Yoknapatawpha Country*, 248. If [Ike] had understood the story from the "old times" which he cherished, he might have had the son he desired—or else more sense than to expect to get one after he has turned away from his devoir. His wife's attitude toward him (recorded on pp. 311-315 of *Go Down, Moses*) is apparently very like his mother's toward his father.

just punishment for doctrinaire bachelorhood.[171] Yet, had his son done as well in his compromise with life, *Go Down, Moses* would be an altogether different book.[172]

---

171   Actually, the entire story of "Was," not just its central episode, has to do with the danger of defying nature. It begins and ends with Buck trying to run a fox into the house with hounds. Buddy is incensed at this innocence. And just before Buck is caught "in the henhouse" (i.e., like a foolish fox), he gets himself bowled over and his hip pocket filled with bits of broken whiskey bottle, forgetting something "even a little child would have known: not ever to stand right in front of or right behind a nigger when you scare him...." (19).

172   The connection of Ike McCaslin with this story of the education of his father and uncle is not casually intended by Faulkner. The function of pp. 3-4 of *Go Down, Moses* is, at once, to define Ike as one who misjudges his personal heritage and to identify him as the formal protagonist of the entire suite of stories to follow. In a more inclusive sense, the protagonist is really "McCaslin," or the idea that family could (and should) repre-sent—just as "Sartoris," the idea and family, is the protagonist of *The Unvanquished*; I have given some exposition of that idea in "Brotherhood in 'The Bear': An Exemplum for Critics," *Modern Age*, X (1966), 278-281, and in "The Winding Horn: Hunting and the Making of Men in Faulkner's 'Race at Morning'" (included in the present volume, chap. 6). On the responsibility of Ike and the rest of the McCaslins to the "place" into which they were born Andrew Lytle has written that Ike is "the exemplum of the Puritan hero, who holds in fee simple the body of the world, and who is incapable, as are all men, of this responsibility" ("The Son of Man: He will Prevail," *The Sewanee Review*, LXIII [1955], 127-128.) I contend that Faulkner's point in "Was" as elsewhere, is that capable or not, man must test himself and to be tested in responsibility. To fulfill himself, he must en-dure, in pride and humility, land, women and position—all.

10.

On the Importance of Discovering God: Faulkner and Hemingway's "The Old Man and the Sea"[173]

William Faulkner did not often pass public judgment on the productions of other authors. It is true that he did sprinkle his numerous interviews with comments on literature, new and old; for his habit was to use analogy in discussing his vocation and advising others concerning its practice. Moreover, he liked to be generous and under certain congenial circumstances to pontificate a bit now and again. However, the intent of these references was usually casual and not critical. Apart from a few things done in his professional nonage and comments on Erich Maria Remarque's *The Road Back* (1931) and Jimmy Collins' *Test Pilot* (1931)[174] he wrote only one genuine book review, just a paragraph in length, which appeared in *Shenandoah* in the Fall of 1952.[175] It does not pretend to be an

---

173   This essay was first published in *The Mississippi Quarterly*, Vol. 20, No. 3 (Summer 1967), 158-163.

174   The review of the Collins novel was published in *The New Republic* (May 20, 1931). The review is of special interest because Faulkner was himself a pilot and his aviation novel *Pylon*, about a group of barnstormers, was published in 1935, just a few years after the review of *Test Pilot*. [Ed.]

175   All of these reviews are conveniently reprinted in James's Meriwether's collection: *William Faulkner: Essays, Speeches, and Public Letters* (New York: Random House, 1965); the comments on the Remarque novel appear on pp. 185-88; the examination of Collins on pp. 188-92; and the review of *The Old Man and the Sea*, 193.

analysis of its subject, Ernest Hemingway's last published novel. For the piece is otherwise intended. Faulkner on *The Old Man and the Sea*[176] (appearing only a few months after Scribner's issued the novel) is a personal document as well as an exercise in commentary: something like a letter, both to his fellow novelist and the literate world at large, and, like most good letters, more significant for what it tells us about its originator than as a revelation concerning its addressee. Yet it is not to be taken as casual. On few other occasions does the Mississippi novelist spell out more of the assumptions concerning the human dilemma and the most appropriate method for contending with it ... than he does in this brief admiring of what another craftsman made. The most important portion of the *Shenandoah* notice reads as follows:

> This time, he [Hemingway] discovered God, a Creator. Until now, his men and women had made themselves, shaped themselves out of their own clay; their victories and defeats were at the hands of each other, just to prove to themselves or one another how tough they could be. But this time, he wrote about pity: about something somewhere that made them all: the old man who had to catch the fish and then lose it, the fish that had to be caught and then lost, the sharks which had to rob the old man of his fish; made them all and loved them all and pitied them all. It's all right.

In substance, what Faulkner praises in *The Old Man and the Sea* is the shadowing forth in its fable of an attitude toward the order of Creation, toward the arrangement of providentially assigned roles within that order, and toward the necessity for submission, courtesy, and mutual respect between creatures disposed within that arrangement to its all-sustaining operation—a sense of transcendent

---

Faulkner repeated his judgement of the Hemingway novel in later recorded conversations at the University of Virginia (*Faulkner in the University* [Charlottesville: University of Virginia Press, 1959], eds. Frederick L. Gwynn and J.L. Blotner, 149 and 161).

176 *The Old Man and the Sea* (New York: Scribner's, 1952).

"pity" contained in pattern, parts, and their interaction. In other words, what delights him is a fresh affinity between Hemingway's "philosophy"—his view of man's place as a contingency among contingencies, a small component in the frame of things which he must recognize and confront if he is to be complete—and the Doctrine of Nature which undergirds the Yoknapatawpha books.

For Faulkner the intransigent and mysterious face of the physical universe is, in all its intellectually irreducible particularity, "an objective correlative for that in man's life which is given, *a priori*, 'other,' for that with which man must come to terms in 'Pride and Humility.'[177] The Creation, in some of its aspects, implies the "Creator." So Faulkner reasons. From evidence of the loving evocation of the violent and circuitous dialectic of Hemingway's microcosm, he discovers a deference to the "something somewhere that made ... [and meaningfully distributed] all." But "discovering God" (a numinous, basically unknowable Jehovah) is not all he believes Hemingway has done. Several responses to a "Creator" are possible, especially for people who once believed "they shaped themselves out of their own clay," or that "their defeats and victories were [only] at the hands of each other." *The Old Man and the Sea,* Faulkner believes, contains the right one. The Southerner may have misunderstood this aquatic *heldenleben* of his most prestigious American contemporary. Certainly, he ignores some of its overtones. Nothing is said of the old fisherman's effect on the boy Manolo, which we would have expected to please him. Neither does he remark the importance which Santiago attaches to his having gone out "too far."

---

177 See "Escaping Westward: Faulkner's 'Golden Land,'" [included in the present volume, chap. 3]. On the central importance of the "endurance" theme to Faulkner's achievement, see "Faulkner's 'Tall Men,'" "'Tomorrow' and the Plain People," "'Spotted Horses' and the Short Cut to Paradise: A Note on the Endurance Theme in Faulkner," "The Gum Tree Scene in Faulkner's 'The Bear,'" and "The Winding Horn: Hunting and the Making of Men in Faulkner's 'Race at Morning'"—all included in the present volume. See also "Brotherhood in 'The Bear': An Exemplum for Critics" (*Modern Age*, X [Summer 1966], 278-81; and "Faulkner, James Baldwin, and the South" (*Georgia Review*, XX [Winter 1966], 431-43.

But Faulkner does not fail to accomplish what he intends. His review goes to the heart of what sets off Hemingway's "romance" from the rest of his work: its piety, its freedom from the rebellious Prometheanism and fatalism of the humanists and/or naturalists. Many characters in the Hemingway novels of the twenties, thirties, and forties do seem either to have "made themselves" or to live only to protest against what they *were* made. Neither the tone of their depiction nor the patterns of their fortune speak to the contrary.... For them the overarching backdrop, the "set" inside of which they play out a scene, is (if suggested at all) merely a hostile, unrelated "it." With them nothing of the difficulty the flesh is heir to as an inevitable part of mortality is affirmed—nothing of the machinery for testing or the supervision of that machinery's functioning by a brooding "Arbiter." But not so with the ancient mariner of the last book. There's a difference in *The Old Man and the Sea*, something not in most other Hemingway: the mood of acceptance and beatitude communicated despite (even through) all the conflicting "had to's," the counterpart of the serenity of Faulkner's hunters and woodmen, ladies and gentlemen, farmers and soldiers (of both races) who balance in themselves antipodal aggressive and fatalistic impulses in order to "cope" with a world whose justice or morality is unavailable to their comprehension.

In Santiago's experience the northern novelist gave perceptive readers reason to believe that he had found his way to a hard truth, acquired what were for him new "bearings." This is what Faulkner meant in declaring what Hemingway had "discovered God." And by so declaring while at the same time extolling the tale of the great fish as his rival's "best," Faulkner indicated (in the Old Testament idiom he usually fell into when giving serious utterance to his *Weltanschauung*) that there is a connection between the excellence of the novel in question and the "discovery" it projects. We could have no better proof that something like this sense of an inscrutable but pitying Order-Giver went into Faulkner's work as a self-conscious part of its development—no better evidence that something like an intimation of Providence is part of the envelope within which it unfolds.

Santiago is the double of the Faulkner hero who, too proud to rest passive but too humble to imagine that he can reshape the world, is at peace once he (in the Mississippian's favorite normative expression) "does the best he can." [When he fails] to bring back to Cuba the marlin he caught, he doesn't blame his failure on the malice of the gods or the misdeeds of men. Like Faulkner's Ewings in "Golden Land,"[178] he "gained a strange peace through fortitude and the will and strength to endure." He knows that it is the part of sharks to raven as it is of men (despite the incidental opposition of elements and creatures) to fish and to strive to display evidence of what their skill, strength, and courage bring, as it is of the leviathans of the deep (the game who are their immediate adversaries) to test and resist them. Given, in his last years, one final chance to prove himself (a chance all the more weighted because of the handicaps that hedge it round about), the Cuban is restored by his adventure and is secure in his manhood with its conclusion—secure even though his triumph is, practically speaking, abortive. The important thing for all (fisherman, game fish, predator) is that they make a run in the "steeplechase," perform their nature, prove (as does the little hound bitch in "The Bear" who finds the courage to go in "once" on Old Ben) that they have a right to be numbered among the respectable representatives of their own kind.[179] Victory is not important; endurance, properly understood, is. God rewards it (and nothing else) well—with what Faulkner calls, in this review, "pity" (an inner grace, not an outward gesture of favor).[180] And man applauds it, must applaud it! For from no other discipline grows the not at all abstract "brotherhood of finitude," the awareness of a common mortal lot which engenders in those who

---

178   "Golden Land" appears on pp. 701-26 of Faulkner's *Collected Stories* (New York: Random House, 1950).

179   The events to which I refer are found on p. 199 of *Go Down, Moses* (New York: Random House, 1942).

180   For Ike McCaslin's overt assertion that the ways of God are just and Creation good, see *Go Down, Moses*, 348-49. His remark includes reference to a variety of interlocking and distinctive but interdependent roles such as Faulkner discovers in Hemingway's novel: the idea of the world as a proving ground or "vale of soul-making." The theory is commonplace in Faulkner. For other expressions of it see *The Big Woods* (New York: Random House, 1955), 168-71; "Race at Morning," 188; and *Go Down, Moses*, 191-92.

accept and confront it as "given" all the traits that lend meaning and dignity to their own and (by imputation) others' lives. Only among the enduring is community possible.

As Faulkner sees it, such is the burden and the importance of *The Old Man and the Sea*. He finds no fear in the book, no resentment, despair, or ennui—only a word "to help man endure by lifting his heart." Hence Faulkner makes an exception of his rule to endorse it in print. The novel conforms to the just quoted prescription for modern writers in the Nobel Prize address of 1950.

Faulkner's one review also does, in a minimum of space, a fine job of translating its subject's structure into expository terms. It is an example of the kind of leap in illumination that has been so difficult for critics who have its author as theirs.[181] Hemingway's book, naturally a puzzle and a disappointment to certain admirers of his earlier works, "recommends" what it depicts. Apparently, Faulkner felt some impulse to tell us that it did even more, that he was willing to let it do some talking for him. And with the assistance the *Shenandoah* note gives us in uncovering his metaphysic and in piecing together the system subsumed in the innocuous terms in which he prefers to couch that vision, perhaps we might do better with the explication of Faulkner's own fiction, imitate his performance, and ascertain just what his counsel is.

---

181   Bradford's meaning here is obscure, but the wording has been left as it appears in the original publication. To judge by the sentence that follows, possibly he is referring to critics who *claim* Hemingway as "theirs." [Ed.]

11.

Family and Community in Faulkner's "Barn Burning"[182]

"**B**arn Burning" is in several different respects a very important story.[183] For one thing, it is well made—by general agreement, one of Faulkner's best short fictions. It is also a gloss on the entire Snopes trilogy, for which it was originally designed to serve as an opening episode or "overture." And finally it was chosen by its author for the first place in his *Collected Stories*:[184] chosen to introduce certain major themes which are in evidence throughout the collection. "Barn Burning" is reported by a forceful third person, with assistance from sections of objective narration and bits of dramatic dialogue. The protagonist is Colonel Sartoris "Sarty" Snopes, an extraordinary boy who is the young son of Abner Snopes, the head of that despicable clan.[185] The narrative focuses on this boy and is the issue of a conflict between son and father. Here is rendered

---

182   This essay was first published in *The Southern Review*, Vol. 17, No. 2 (Spring 1981), 332-339.

183   "Barn Burning was first published in *Harper's Magazine* (June 1939), 86-96.

184   *Collected Stories of William Faulkner* (New York: Random House, 1950), 3-25.

185   The Snopes, for the uninitiated reader, are the largest of Yoknapatawpha's clans. Some 67 characters in Faulkner's fiction bear the Snopes name. The lawyer Gavin Stevens, in the second volume of what is termed the "Snopes Trilogy," says of them: "They were just Snopes, like colonies of rats or termites." *The Town* (New York: Random House, 1957), 39. [Ed.]

briefly, and with masterful pacing, the painful and hasty maturation of a fine young man. Tension builds and is then resolved in the context of his special personality. In the course of the story Sarty becomes what his given name suggests, a supporter of that larger family that is community and a protector of right order. Yet that identity is a contradiction of everything else that [the name] Snopes comes to signify in the trilogy. We can understand why Faulkner finally decided not to use this material to begin *The Hamlet*. There is too much distance between Sarty and most of his kindred. Such a prologue might confuse the reader, prepare him for things that do not follow. But we must also recognize that if Sarty is the best of all his kind, out of place [among the Snopes], his father (or his respect for what the *concept* "father" suggests) helped to make him so. And we should remember that his rejection of mere blood loyalty is only a partial contradiction of that imperative, of the social structure within which it is presupposed.

In interpreting this narrative, we should begin by examining as a progression the sequence of episodes which gives to it a structure and a point. First comes an abortive hearing before a rustic Justice of the Peace, the resolution of a dispute between Abner Snopes and a hapless neighbor. A barn has been burned. Its owner, Mr. Harris, demands redress. There is no solid evidence that a Snopes was involved in this conflagration. All that can be proved is that Abner was angry when Harris penned up his stray hog and demanded a pound fee of one dollar for its return. But the community, represented by the magistrate, must hear out Harris' explosion of anger and reflect their agreement with it. For they know the story of what passed between him and the hog's neglectful owner. And they can see the probabilities inscribed in the solemn, stiff, and angry appearance of the black-coated Mr. Snopes. Yet they are not vengeful—not like Abner. They will not put the barn burner's youngest son to a question he cannot easily answer. It is enough that they be rid of this source of disorder in their midst and that they leave no doubt in the mind of the arsonist as to whom they blame for Harris' fire. Sarty is told that no one believes that a boy with "Colonel Sartoris" as his given name would lie. Prudence, mercy, and the law dissolve his dilemma. Sarty, Abner, and the unnamed older brother join their family in a wagon.

There is a rapid departure. And after a little travel they are relocated in their new home, a nondescript sharecropper's cabin much like the one they had just left—or perhaps a trifle worse.

The morning after the reestablishment of the Snopes family, Abner takes Sarty with him to meet the new landlord: [Major de Spain] the man who, as Snopes has said the evening before, "aims to begin tomorrow owning me body and soul for the next eight months." Sarty is calmed and lifted in spirit by the majestic air and beauty of the De Spain mansion. Abner is merely irritated. Instead of being caught by its "spell," he wants only to put his mark upon the great white house. On purpose, he tracks in manure on an expensive rug. The Major sends it out to be cleaned and restored by those who soiled it. Abner then compounds his original insult by ruining the rug altogether. Once again, Snope's conflict is thrown before a local magistrate. De Spain asks that his loss be made good—at least in proportion to Abner's probable income. But only a very moderate restitution is required of the always angry tenant. Abner, however, will not submit to even a mild correction—not until he can say of the encounter, "I had them beat." He makes preparations to seek a justice of his own, preparations which Sarty cannot misunderstand. Driven to a choice between antipodal, exaggerated alternatives—the risk of indirect patricide, or a blind loyalty to tribe, whatever it may cost—the boy takes the former option and, in respect for self and others, breaks away to warn De Spain that Abner is on his way. After rousing the planter, the boy then hurries to check his "pap." But he appears to be too late. There is a glare from the outbuildings. De Spain rides by him, toward the fire. Shots follow. From shouting, flames, and tumult, young Snopes flees. But he carries with him, as he disappears, a selective memory of "father," a still-needed foundation for the life he will make for himself. The story closes on a lyric, tranquil note as Sarty pauses on a hilltop, regards the slow but steady revolution of the stars, sleeps a bit, and later awakens to the choiring of birds. Then as the morning comes, he moves from our ken, down toward a line of trees.

There is a great economy of action and characterization in this progression, and it is marched with a careful control of tone. Structure is reinforced by rhythm and imagery. In consequence, the burden of this narrative is almost unmistakable. Abner Snopes is the antagonist. The fierce and implacable emotions which drive him toward ruin are revealed to us as to his youngest son. Yet as Abner moves, stage by stage, toward a break with Sarty, the boy tries harder and harder to persuade himself that his father will change, will be "satisfied" and shake off his incendiary compulsions. However, Faulkner also lets us know that the barn burner will not turn aside and that it is inevitable that Sarty will be forced to go with him, or against.

There is, of course, no extrinsic explanation of the rectitude of Colonel Sartoris Snopes. What the authoritative narrator tells us about the operation of Sarty's mind gives us no latitude for simplistic determinisms. Nor do we get anything to that effect from occasional drafts upon his adult consciousness or from the record of this conduct. He is simply one of Faulkner's enduring, in rebellion against nothing that is given, nothing that fails within the scope of his responsibility. Even after he thinks that he has killed Abner,[186] he first cries "Pap" and then adds "Father"—for the person, but also for the role or principle Abner was supposed to perform. Nothing less than what the elder Snopes persists in doing could have moved the boy to take any action against him. And even his warning to De Spain does not change his commitment to the patriarchal imperative, his need for a usable past, a patrimony. For it is individual self-respect or honor which requires loyalty to the family bond, the source of identity, not the other way around. Community is the natural consequence of the presence in society of many decent men and women, not a guarantee that such persons will appear. Devotion to a dream of "peace and dignity" when the necessary human raw materials are

---

186   Readers will recall that shortly after Sarty shouts his warning to De Spain, he hears gunshots. The tragic tone of the passage and Sarty's use of the past tense in reference to his father both strongly hint not only that Abner has been killed but that Sarty understands this and holds himself accountable. No evidence that Abner did, in fact, die, is presented in the text, but we can be sure that for Sarty, speaking psychologically and morally, his father, if not the ideal of fatherhood, is dead. [Ed.]

missing, where there are no good stewards asking "only truth, justice,"[187] is an exercise in futility. Therefore, when Sarty connects his name with the cherished myth of Abner's military service to the Confederacy, he is only affirming the part of his father which comes closest to the standard of personal and family honor, the notion of social order resting on a base of exchanged respect and mutual interdependence, that Colonel John Sartoris[188] had epitomized. Neither name nor memory is an explanation of his private moral sense, though both may have reinforced it. Or perhaps it is better to say that they provided an idiom for its expression. The fact that Sarty is wrong when he cries to himself. "He was brave! He was in the war! He was in Colonel Sartoris' cav'ry!"[189] only underscores our sense of his moral independence, his faith in the principles of fatherhood, however some fathers may offend against it, and however he may condemn their failures.

But independence aside, it is nonetheless true that Sarty organizes his feelings about Abner's war against an "offending" world, and prepares to set himself apart from that war, in response to positive experiences and images that confront him in the course of "Barn Burning," most particularly in reaction to the "spell" of "peace and joy" which comes over him when he stands between two brick pillars and has a first glimpse of the De Spain house. There, for a moment, he "forgot his father and the terror"—the fear that he will be drawn after his father in "the old fierce pull of blood,"[190] in "the old habit, the old blood which he had not been permitted to choose for himself, which had been bequeathed him willy nilly and which had run for so long (and who knew where, battening of what of outrage and savagery and lust) before it came to him."[191] Though Sarty notes the size of the house ("Hit's big as a courthouse"), it is

---

187   *Collected Stories*, 8.

188   In Faulkner's fiction, Col. John Sartoris was a Civil War hero who led a unit of Partisan Rangers in raids against the invading Union Army. He was the founder of the Sartoris dynasty in Yoknapatawpha County.[Ed.]

189   *Collected Stories*, 24.

190   *Collected Stories*, 3.

191   *Collected Stories*, 21.

not De Spain's wealth that moves him. Neither is he admiring *as power, for power's sake*, the influence over men which the mansion implies. Certainly, he is not admiring of De Spain as a person. For the Major, though a decent man, is nothing special—not a Colonel John Sartoris. Rather, it is an image of civility that the De Spain house speaks to the Snopes boy. Beauty is part of that impression, a beauty which includes De Spain's wife—the first "lady" Sarty has ever seen. And manners—precisely the value Abner negates in soiling the rug. In English literature the "great house" image has functioned in this way since the seventeenth century. It is present in several of Faulkner's novels. It does not *make* the protagonist of this story try to be a gentleman. Instead, it elicits from him an awareness of his *already present inclination* to act that part. To the same effect are Sarty's two encounters with local courts and the patience of Abner's two "adversaries," Harris and De Spain—to say nothing of the generous influences of the boy's mother and his aunt. Sarty can find around him embodiments of how he wants to behave. But the disposition in that direction, and the resistance to his father's example, are antecedent to his discovery of such models, though their courtesy and charity may speed up the process which separates him from Snopes.

That all sorts of good, responsible, and reasonable people (and the best things these people have made and preserved) should have a positive purchase on a young boy growing up is only natural in a deferential society. Together they say to him, "Do the best you can," or "Be the best that you can be." Yet as I have already argued, the chief influence on Colonel Sartoris Snopes is a negative one, a force against which he defines himself. To understand the tendency of that negative force, it is necessary to examine, in the context of his world and its particular history, the character of Abner Snopes. In simple terms, Abner is envy incarnate. Yet this language is not precisely adequate. For Abner does not wish to acquire anything enjoyed by those who offend him. His trouble is that he has experienced the contempt of those whose regard he had once desired. And he continues to find evidence of such contempt on every pretext imaginable. His is therefore the kind of envy that results in hatred and malicious deeds—all of them performed in the name of injured merit and a private sense of justice. It is an inverted form of respect which requires the degradation of things he is too proud to want and persons whose values he cannot reproduce. His principal reminder of past humiliation is with him everywhere: a stiff leg, injured by a Confederate provost's musket ball trying to steal southern horses. He is thus a lesser (and southern) representative of the breed we know best through Melville's Captain Ahab and Aeschylus' Prometheus or through Satan of *Paradise Lost*.

Other aspects of Abner's appearance also bespeak his nature. We should look closely at the imagery employed by Faulkner to help us visualize what he is. First, he is called "wolflike" and driven by "a ferocious conviction of the rightness of his own actions."[192] We are somewhat reminded of his kinsman, Mink Snopes, in *The Hamlet* and *The Mansion*. However, though Abner is a formidable man in a warped and terrifying way, his fury does not result in the ordinary gestures of outrage. Mink does his business with a gun, in broad daylight. In contrast, Abner enjoys darkness, stealth, and the fear that fire by night can produce. This is not simply a difference in bravery or in the strategies of revenge. The distinction is more fundamental. For, as Sarty understands, "the element of fire spoke to some deep mainspring of his father's being."[193] It is not precisely that Abner worships fire (the power of destruction) or the forces of evil or that he is (as were his prototypes) in ontological rebellion against the disposing powers themselves. But Snopes's resentment of the minimal terms of social coexistence is so intense as to amount to little less than a quarrel with the gods. Certainly, he is dehumanized by his ruling passion. In the presence of the De Spain mansion (or any other form of excellence), he is "ravening and jealous rage" in an "iron-like black coat." His is the kind of pride rejected by Christ in Luke 12:13-15: "And one of the company said unto him, Master, speak to my brother, that he divide the inheritance with me. And he said unto him, Man, who made me a judge or a divider over you? And he said unto them, Take heed and beware of covetousness."

---

192   *Collected Stories*, 7.

193   *Collected Stories*, 7.

Justice, and misunderstandings of the term—that is, what does or does not constitute its sphere and its objective character—is a major theme of "Barn Burning." The very real justice of Harris and the rural magistrate in the first trial scene, when taken in conjunction with the moderation of De Spain and the Peace Justice of his county (who awards the planter only ten bushels of corn for his rug), marks how little is required of Abner—at least in comparison with what might be imposed upon him if those involved thought of punishment as an end in itself. True, the dignity and authority of the law is preserved. The letter is honored. But the justice accepted by these men weighs circumstance. In addition, it considers what the application of the law in all its rigor might do to them and to their communities. They do not invoke it in order to "get the best of" or "beat" their adversaries. Abner, in contrast, thinks of the law only in terms of conflict and advantage. If he cannot prove what he is worth through recourse to legal proceedings, he will prove it on his own, according to his personal ideal of justice. And that ideal isolates him. He is clearly a mechanical creature, minus ordinary human feelings for either man or beast. "Bloodless," "stiff," and "implacable,"[194] he seems hardly human. Twice we are told of his figure that it is depthless, "as though cut from tin."[195] We might well be reminded of Talus, the metallic, merciless avenger in Book V of Spenser's *Faerie Queene*, and of certain other denatured or "monstrous" figures appearing elsewhere in the Faulkner corpus. Abner's justice is revenge for imagined injuries—making others pay for the fact that he is Abner Snopes, and sometimes recognized for what he is. Despite the name he gave the boy and regardless of whatever myths of the past he gave to Sarty which nourished youthful self-respect, the barn burner does not seem to care for any work. Delight in honorable labor, whatever is "within his scope" and some "beyond it," is a quality in his youngest son. But Sarty "had this from his mother." Nor, despite his talk of blood, does Abner exhibit even a modicum of family feeling. His only emotion is cold anger. And it is difficult for a father so eaten up by rage to preserve any hold on his children.

_____

194   *Collected Stories*, 10.

195   *Collected Stories*, 10.

Earlier in the story, before coming to the De Spain plantation, Abner has recognized that Sarty does not share his animus against an offending world and that the boy is reluctant to lie for him. Abner is correct in his assessment. A key passage confirming his suspicions comes in the opening scene. Sarty is called forward to tell what he knows of the fire in the Harris barn. He is in a daze, full of "despair" and "grief." The boy has told himself, "He aims for me to lie. And I will have to do hit."[196] Then, as Harris is asked if he really wants the boy to testify against his father, there is a moment's silence: "it was as if he had swung outward, at the end of a grape vine, over a ravine, and at the top of the swing had been caught at a prolonged instant of mesmerized gravity, weightless in time."[197] The image suggests both relief and peril. And also something else. To be suspended over a ravine by a slender cord is a figure for Sarty's tenuous connection with his family. And to be without blood kindred is to fall, dreadfully, in space. But to be weightless is to be free of the force that pulls a man below his mark. It is liberation from the burden of an evil heritage. Yet there is also exhilaration in such freedom. Abner has put him in this place: Abner and the measured, prudent behavior of the communities Abner invades. When the stiff-legged man in the long black coat decides to do a bit of his burning at the De Spain place, he offends something fundamental in his son's identity. And thus snaps the cord.

These materials are brought together with overwhelming unity of effect. The conclusion of "Barn Burning" brings a remarkable release of tension—almost a catharsis—which is a consequence of the reader's participation in the internal conflict of Sarty, the unnatural and hyperbolic choice he is forced to make. Blood loyalty and the social principle are ordinarily inseparable. But, to make a point, Faulkner takes us outside of ordinary experience. In the equation, familial/social, he forces us to ask which is the end and which the means. That Abner is inhuman, almost one-dimensional, makes it easier for the author to focus narrowly on Sarty's consciousness, to insist that the moral life is finally a question of internal choice. Sarty

---

196   *Collected Stories*, 4.

197   *Collected Stories*, 5.

and Abner both look like victims to sentimental modern readers. Therefore, the release provided by Sarty's race to warn De Spain is hard for them to acknowledge. Old language, in this situation, will serve us best. Abner is pride alone, with no humility. He is devoured by pride's corrosive force. He rejects the providential, denies the primacy of the social bond. In contrast, his son lives *with* and *out of* the given. Though an independent moral force, all the more splendid in this degrading context, Sarty defines his situation *within* history and responds to kindness, to beauty, and to whatever good examples he can find, reaching out to what answers best to his essential self. Hence, he does more than just "withdraw" from Snopes. Rather, he sorts out certain parts of his heritage from other elements he cannot use. In the terms Faulkner uses to judge Isaac McCaslin of *Go Down, Moses*, Sarty says, "I'm going to do something about it." This is what makes of his experience, as rendered in this wonderfully made narrative, so appropriate an introduction to Faulkner's *Collected Stories*.

12.

Faulkner's "A Courtship": An Accommodation of Cultures[198]

Some of William Faulkner's finest short stories (to say nothing of sections in several of his novels) are concerned with the native American inhabitants of his portion of Mississippi and with the decline and collapse of their ancient culture. These self-contained fictions treat of this time of transition and of the Indian leaders responsible for the decline of the red man and his replacement by new settlers of European stock. We think immediately of "Red Leaves." Poor leadership and corruption from without are issues there. But the most impressive of these tales, "A Justice," recounts the story of the last and worst of these chieftains, the one called Doom once he becomes the tribal patriarch, but known before as Ikkemotubbe.[199] Other stories in this set have merits of their own. My subject is one of these.

"A Courtship"[200] depicts an early time in the life of Ikkemotubbe and a different relation between Indian and white man than what

---

198   This essay was originally published in *The South Atlantic Quarterly*, Vol. 80, No. 3 (Summer 1981) by Duke University Press, 355-59.

199   "Red Leaves" and "A Justice" can both be found in *Collected Stories of William Faulkner* (New York: Random House, 1955)—the first on pp. 313-41; the second on pp. 343-60.

200   *Collected Stories,* 361-80—first written in 1942 but not published until six years later by *Sewanee Review* (Spring 1948).

we observe in its companion stories. Though in time of composition and publication the latest of Faulkner's narratives of "the Old People,"[201] it represents Saxon/Celt intrusion into the Chickasaw/Choctaw world in a more positive light than do these closely related fictions. It functions as a counterpoint to these tales, to portions of certain novels, and especially to "A Justice." Indeed, its relation to these materials is almost normative. We therefore do well to look at it closely.

The speaker in "A Courtship" is an Indian. As was the case in "A Justice," what we hear may be the voice of Sam Fathers (better known to us in *Go Down, Moses*) speaking to the young Quentin Compson.[202] For once again the talk is of "how it was in the old days." With that motif this story begins and ends. It is a narrative answer to an implicit question. Things were better in that other time. Chickasaw relations with the American government had been regularized, boundaries had been established, and "sticks burned" to formalize the understanding. In one nation Andrew Jackson was "the Man." In the other, old Issetibbeha still reigned, "so old that nothing more was required of him except to sit in the sun and criticize the degeneration of the People and the folly and rapacity of politicians."[203] But what really gives to "A Courtship" a nostalgic substance is its central image, of the friendship of Ikkemotubbe and David Hogganbeck, the huge river pilot, who competes with the old

---

201 Faulkner included Indian characters and themes in roughly a dozen texts between 1930 and 1957. Along with the three stories already mentioned, the story "Lo!" (1934) can be found in the *Collected Stories*. One may also find treatments of the Indians in "The Bear Hunt" (1934), "The Old People" (1940), *Go Down, Moses* (1942), and *The Town* (1957), just to name the most prominent. Bradford's essay "Faulkner and the Great White Father," included in the present volume (Chap. 2), focuses on "Lo!"

202 The auditor to whom Sam Fathers tells this tale is not named, but is most likely Quentin Compson at a young age, to judge by the references to Jason and Caddy, Quentin's brother and sister, in the opening paragraph. Quentin is a principal character in the novels *The Sound and the Fury* (1929) and *Absalom, Absalom!* (1936). Sam Fathers is the son of a Chickasaw Indian father and a slave mother, and appears in several of Faulkner's stories and novels, but principally in "A Justice" and "The Old People" (first published in 1940 but then revised and included in *Go Down, Moses*).

203 *Collected Stories*, 362.

chieftain's nephew, the one whom the People "loved the best," for the hand of an Indian maiden, the placid but beautiful sister of Herman Basket[204]–a bronze version of Eula Varner.[205]

To make certain that we recognize the importance of this nostalgic core in "A Courtship" and to ensure that we remember other less genial patterns of intercultural contact that are possible, Faulkner enforces its contrapuntal link to "A Justice" with a summary of the later career of Ikkemotubbe as reported in that antecedent work. Faulkner's placement of this material specifies how it is to be construed, for it comes before and after the narrative proper. The digressions concern how Ikkemotubbe became Doom and seized the Manship of his tribe: how he changed in the company of a white friend (the Chevalier Soeur-Blonde de Vitry), "whom no man wished to love,"[206] into an Indian Machiavel. However, if we look closely at the digressions and the story itself, we are not led to believe that what happens to the Indian warrior while he is visiting "down the river" in New Orleans was caused by his unhappy experience with courtship. The vagaries of women are well known among the Chickasaw. And when Hogganbeck and Ikkemotubbe discover that the accord which they have forged from the materials of their contest has been developed almost for nothing, that Herman Basket's sister has chosen for a husband a lazy, nondescript boy called Log-in-the-Creek, their bond in frustration only reinforces their union through competition. The erstwhile rivals leave the Plantation[207] together because they are embarrassed by what the girl has done and unable (for the moment) to live in near proximity to the scene of their disgrace. But all that signifies between them, all that the author has

---

204   Herman Basket, or "Pappy," is, in fact, a Chickasaw Indian and the biological father of Sam Fathers.

205   Eula Varner appears most notably in *The Hamlet* (New York: Random House, 1940), the first of Faulkner's so-called "Snopes Trilogy." In that novel, Faulkner's narrator suggests that she represents "some symbology out of the old Dionysic times—honey in sunlight and bursting grapes ...." (105).

206   "A Courtship," *Collected Stories*, 379.

207   The "Plantation" in this context refers to Chickasaw tribal lands in Mississippi prior to 1832 and the Indian Removal Act. [Ed.]

chosen to emphasize, is settled before they head south, announcing with the "crying-rope" (whistle) of Captain Studenmare's boat the pain of their regret.

Basket's sister is "looked upon" by Ikkemotubbe before Hogganbeck arrives at the Plantation for the annual trading visit of the steamboat. Other Indians had also noticed her, but "looked away" when the Man's nephew, "the best one," came courting. But not the visitor, the young pilot almost twice the size of all the braves. This year he notices the girl he also has overlooked on previous visits, and brings his fiddle to sit on Herman Basket's gallery and make the music. Before the trader's boat "walked" up the river, Ikkemotubbe has already made himself presentable (in a wild motley of formal attire), performing certain feats, and offered presents to Basket and his wife. He cannot brook a rival so formidable as this white man. Therefore he perceives that only victory over Hogganbeck in a fair contest can secure for him the favor of the woman of his choice. That is, unless he wants to kill David. And in his eyes to kill a rival would be a kind of defeat. Says the proud warrior, "If I am to truly win, it will be necessary for you to be there to see it. On the day of the wedding I wish you to be present... ."[208] That kind of desire for honor or esteem in the eyes of an adversary is present from the beginning of this encounter. It produces an exemplary result.

But this is not to say that David and Ikkemotubbe pretend that they are not very different men from very different worlds. A mutual recognition of all that these providential boundaries mean (and do not mean) is a precondition of their precarious but honorable accommodation. It has been a mistake of some earlier comment on this story to find in it a teaching on equality, in the conventional modern sense of the term. The first distinction acknowledged openly by both contestants is that of physical capacity. In this case that distinction is, in part, a matter of race. But even before they have made this gesture, both men have offered a larger (if implicit) concession to difference, a concession that is logically prior to these adjustments with respect to person and origin: David in submitting

_____
208   *Collected Stories*, 371.

to the Indian framework for testing, and Ikkemotubbe is accepting a challenge from the "outside." To be sure, Hogganbeck says something about common denominators in reaching beyond his own race in search of a wife. And, from the very beginning of their connection, his Indian opponent treats him with hospitality and something very like brotherly affection. To keep an eye on each other and prevent suspicion of advantage, taken or received, these young men become inseparable. They sleep in one house, they exchange jests at their own shortcomings, and each salutes what the other achieves as an excellence of its own variety. Ikkemotubbe cannot eat so much as Hogganbeck, or drink so much, or dance so long. The white man cannot race horses or sprint so well as the brave. Nevertheless, these skills are demonstrated by the rivals through unequal contest or unchallenged display, usually arranged for or assented to by the disadvantaged contestant: demonstrated in order that each may, in kind, perform his nature. Only then do they attempt to arrange a contest which balances off their respective capacities. A distance race, they agree, is a contest in which either one might prevail, especially if Hogganbeck's slight disadvantage as a runner is balanced by a challenge to Ikkemotubbe's lesser strength—a challenge which will occur only if he pulls ahead of his powerful opponent.

They agree to settle who is to enjoy the liberty of paying court to Basket's lethargic sister with a run of approximately one hundred and thirty miles, a three-day marathon race to a fabled cave in the isolated country of David Colbert, a mighty chieftain of an earlier time. It was to spend a night in this place that Indian boys went to complete their rites of passage. The one to arrive there first is to enter, fire his pistol, and then withdraw. But there is a problem with this last part of the test. The roof of the cave is ready to collapse. Only a man of superhuman strength is likely to survive its fall. The two contestants have deferred to each other throughout their earlier encounters. They have agreed that there can be no true comparison between "different kinds of best." When their contests seemed to pit "apples against oranges," the winner would say to his adversary, "What do you suggest now?" But with this race, to this conclusion, no deference will be required.

The climax of this action is clearly the distance run. It is reported in an almost heroic vein—in keeping with the high tradition of the Indian narratives of great feats, remembered for the instruction of the young. Ikkemotubbe and Hogganbeck enter together into the brotherhood of the brave, and they begin to call each other by that name. The Indian runs only a little ahead of the white youth. He helps him along the way, giving him food and water when he collapses. And for a time he runs beside him, with a hand on his shoulder. But he reaches the cave first, fires, and is caught by the collapsing roof. Or almost caught. For David was only a few steps behind, and he supports the roof on his back, urging his rival to escape. The Indian then risks his life in turn, crawling out to return, prop the roof with a pole, and drag David out behind him, while the roof continues its fall. Observing this encounter, in conjunction with the rest of their dispute, we can understand why the People "loved David Hogganbeck … as they loved Ikkemotubbe." For "there were men in those days."[209] What we witness here is the brotherhood of warriors and the circumstances under which such bonds were formed. Its significance is not diminished by the anticlimax which follows; only its formal cause is made ironic.

The pistol in the cave, at the end of a race, is to be sure, an image with sexual overtones. The contest to determine who is the better man, conducted under honorable conditions, with each participant doing his best, is traditionally connected with the quest for the regard of women, the ritual mating. But it is a mistake to make too much of the good life, per se. We must translate this figure into rather simple terms: Once you pursue woman … among all the contestable items of value available in this world, you put yourself in the way of risk, in danger of the "roof falling in." This is a familiar theme in the Faulkner canon and in American literature in general.

Both men desire Herman Basket's sister. Both suffer from their passion. Disappointment in love, like the need for courage, and the difficulty of accepting frustration are universal human bonds. They link host and guest, tribal man and adventurer in the practice

---

209   *Collected Stories*, 373.

of *noblesse oblige*, necessary in a world where the ways of men are many and the recognition of real difference a factor wherever justice is attempted. As David says, in these matters "Perhaps there is just one wisdom for all men, no matter who speaks it."[210]

But it is not enough to refuse advantage and to respect the best that others can achieve. It is also necessary, when things do not go well, that we "reconcile" to our failures. Hogganbeck appears to have some of this ability. In any case, he is improved by this time in the Chickasaw world. He learns to endure, to accept what is given with "pride and humility," and to start from where he is. With Ikkemotubbe it may have gone the other way around. He was prepared to lose to David—at least, prepared to lose and die. But Log-in-the-Creek is too much. From such helplessness he may have learned only that he did not want to be so helpless again. Such an interpretation explains the digressions on his later career as Doom included in this story and the tone adopted by the narrator in remembering him as a symbol of "the People" at their best. For the Indian who returns to the Plantation after years in New Orleans will submit to nothing, honor no ruler, extend grace and hospitality to no rival for public esteem. Perhaps he has become the completion of the process which caused his uncle "to criticize the People" for their degeneration in the midst of the Great Spirit's blessings. Apart from the inevitable human difficulties, their yoke was easy. Doom broke the terms of their tenure upon the good land. As he appears in "A Courtship," as *Ikkemotubbe*, he might have forestalled this drift and made an accommodation with the incoming whites which would have preserved the dignity of both peoples and made of their confrontation a benefit to all. Instead, he violated the traditional "way" of his tribe, making of the recollection of his "preconversion, premodern excellence" an all the more pointed account of how it was in those "old and better" days.

---

210 *Collected Stories*, 380.

13.

The Anomaly of Faulkner's
World War I Stories[211]

The seven stories of the Great War which William Faulkner composed in his lifetime, when considered in conjunction with *Soldiers' Pay, Flags in the Dust,* and *A Fable*, his novels of World War I, constitute a sizeable component of his total artistic performance.[212] No separable segment of the Faulkner canon is so large unto itself or so easily set apart with distinctions in tone, theme, and setting. Except in the cases of "Thrift" and "With Caution and Dispatch," what may be said of one of these stories may (usually) be said of all. They belong to a stylized body of literature informed by what Paul

---

211   This essay was first published in *The Mississippi Quarterly*, Vol. 36, No. 3 (Summer 1983), 243-262.

212   Five of these stories appear in *Collected Stories of William Faulkner* (New York: Random House, 1950) in section IV, "The Wasteland": "Ad Astra," Victory," Crevasse," "Turnabout," and "All the Dead Pilots." It should be remembered that Faulkner's first published story, "Landing in Luck," concerned flight training in Canada for the RAF. It originally appeared November 26, 1919, in *The Mississippian* [University of Mississippi] and is reprinted in *William Faulkner: Early Prose and Poetry* (Boston: Little, Brown, and Co., 1962), ed. Carvel Collins. "Thrift" appeared first in *The Saturday Evening Post*, 203, (Sept. 6, 1930), 16-17, 78, 82. "With Caution and Dispatch" first appeared years after the death of its author, in *Esquire,* 92 (Sept. 1979). Both are included in *Uncollected Stories* (New York: Random House, 1979), ed. Joseph Blotner. Some of Faulkner's poems also reflect his preoccupation with World War I—e.g. "The Lilacs" and "November 11," which appear in his second volume of poems, *A Green Bough* (New York: Smith and Haas, 1933).

Fussell has called "the matter of Flanders and Picardy": a corpus produced in the aftermath of (or in response to) the devastating experience of modern, impersonal, and mechanized "total war."[213] The subjects are "all sad young men" forever changed and emptied by their participation in such a struggle. Faulkner's World War I stories were thus, when they were written, eminently "fashionable." Irving Howe has well said that "they are specimens of a class rather than individual works of art."[214]

But there is another reason for treating them as a "matched set." The merits, flaws, and formal peculiarities of the particular stories in this group become evident only against the backdrop of what they represent as a body of work. And the same holds true of the light they shed on major patterns of motive and conduct in the related novels. Moreover, though these stories add little to Faulkner's stature as an artist, they do tell us a great deal about the set of mind, the imaginative resources, upon which that achievement rests.

Because he had been so affected during his youth by the romantic legend of the flying warrior and because he first sought to test his own manhood in the context of that heroic myth, it is not surprising that military pilots receive special emphasis in Faulkner's narratives

---

213 Paul Fussell, *The Great War and Modern Memory* (New York: Oxford University Press, 1975), x. Michael Millgate, in his "Faulkner and the Literature of the First World War," *Mississippi Quarterly*, 26 (Summer 1973), 387-393, reprints a brief essay written by Faulkner in late 1924 or early 1925 [focused] on three characteristic works from this literature. More evidence of his reading in this area—evidence that suggest the derivative quality of some of his fiction dealing with aviation—is developed by Richard T. Dillon in "Some Sources for Faulkner's Version of the First Air War," *American Literature*, 44 (Jan. 1973), 629-637. An early treatment of these stories is Douglas Day's "The War Stories of William Faulkner," *Georgia Review*, 15 (Winter 1961), 385-394. Another important comment is contained in Hans H. Skei's "The Novelist as Short Story Writer: A Study of William Faulkner's Short Stories with Special Emphasis on the Period 1928-1932," (University of Oslo dissertation, 1980), 33-347.

214 Irving Howe, *William Faulkner: A Critical Study* (New York: Random House, 1952), 191. To the same effect is William Van O'Connor's *The Tangled Fire of William Faulkner* (Minneapolis: University of Minnesota Press, 1954), 67. David Perkins observes of World War I poetry in his *A History of Modern Poetry* (Cambridge: Harvard University Press, 1976), 268-269, that the soldier poets would not accept the horrors of the war they knew as a metaphor for life. Rather, they objected to what they saw as foreign to the basic human condition.

of World War I. In 1918 he trained in Canada for service in the Royal Air Force. Later he liked to be thought of as a onetime British pilot. Moreover, he kept alive for years—until it became a source of embarrassment—an inflated version of his adventures in the King's uniform.[215] For a time he owned his own plane. And as late as World War II he spoke of hopes of flying duty as a ferry pilot.[216] In a sense Faulkner never completely recovered from his youthful infatuation with the chivalry of the air. It is possible to see more than a little of his own experience in David Levine, the disappointed young flier in *A Fable* who prepares to shoot himself because he has reached the front just as the fighting ceased.[217] But this is only one ingredient in his serious view of the original flying warriors. For he also recognized, almost from the first, that if air combat was more glamorous and closer to the old military ethic of significant individual deeds than the harsh reality of the trenches, the futility of this war and the disenchantment produced by waking from these dreams of glory were bound to engender a sharper pain, a deeper revulsion against the waste of life than those felt by the ordinary, illusion-free foot soldier.

Though the World War I stories had been written years before, Faulkner remembered well enough their dominant motif when asked about them in his University of Virginia interviews in the late 1950s. Of the veterans appearing in his fiction, Faulkner remarked, "most of them would have been better off if they had died on the eleventh of November ...." for "in a way they were dead, they had exhausted themselves psychically."[218] These "living dead" are central symbols

---

215 See Joseph Blotner's *Faulkner: A Critical Study* (New York: Random House, 1974), 206-230 and 1202-1203.

216 See *Selected Letters of William Faulkner*, ed. Joseph Blotner (New York: Random House, 1977), 167.

217 *A Fable* (New York: Random House, 1954), 86-120; 323-326. Gerald David Levine is an equivalent of Julian Lowe in *Soldier's Pay* (New York: Boni and Liveright, 1926), 45-46, 52, a young cadet distressed because he reached the war too late to fly in combat.

218 *Faulkner in the University*, ed. Frederick L. Gwynn and Joseph L. Blotner (Charlottesville: University of Virginia Press, 1959), 23, 48.

in *Soldier's Pay* and *Flags in the Dust*; Donald Mahon[219] and Bayard Sartoris the younger clearly belong to their company. They appear in "Honor"[220] and in most of the stories directly concerned with the Great War. And the characters who are still surviving at the end of *A Fable* lead us to believe that it will not be easy for them to avoid the same state. But in the Faulkner canon the story "Ad Astra" is the *locus classicus* for the expression of the theme.

"Ad Astra" documents this emotional shift as it occurs among experienced aviators—fliers of many origins. The time of the story is at the very end of the war. The subjects have—all of them—learned that none of their efforts really counted for much. They form a kind of travelling party or moving conversation. Yet none of them, except their German prisoner and the one non-aviator in the group, the Indian subadar major of native troops, really communicates with his companions by way of words.[221] Rather they affirm a kind of unity through the ritual of drink and through brief, unrelated remarks which they seem to address to themselves, each one speaking in his turn. The opening line of the story specifies their condition: "I don't

---

219   Donald Mahon is the almost passive central figure in *Soldier's Pay*. As one "reacting to" rather than "acting upon," he is Faulkner's first fictional version of the returned warrior as one of the "living dead." A victim of the war, consumed in the air in a moment of dreadful intensity, he is left alive as a graceful husk. Young Bayard Sartoris in *Flags in the Dust* (New York: Vintage, 1974) is a more representative damaged hero, feeling guilty about his own survival. Throughout most of the novel, Bayard is one of the "living dead," with only an "illusion of quickness" (369). His wife could taste on his lips only "fatality and doom" (323). The Mississippi boy has been distracted by watching his twin brother die in combat—and by his own helplessness to prevent John's death. The relationship between this novel and the short stories of World War I is extremely close. See also *Flags in the Dust* (44-47 and 133).

220   "Honor" appears in *Collected Stories* (551-564). The action of the story is affected by the code of Worlds War I aviators, though the war itself is only briefly recalled. The protagonist, Monaghan, sees himself as one of the romantically doomed living dead (562).

221   Carvel Collins, in "Faulkner's War Service and His Fiction," an unpublished paper paraphrased in Blotner (*Biography*, 42-43; 205), tells us that Faulkner met the originals of the subadar and perhaps of the captured German aviator at Yale in 1918. "Ad Astra" was first published in *American Caravan IV*, ed. Alfred Kreymborg, Lewis Mumford, and Paul Rosenfield (New York: Macaulay, 1931), 164-181.

know what we were."[222] Their home and family have been the military service. But instead of giving them identity, their experience of the profession of arms has taken their identity away. Though all but the prisoner are in British uniform, their only fatherland is the other shore of Lethe, where their fallen comrades await their coming. The subadar and the German pilot, noblemen in their own countries but akin in their rejection of the kind of nationalism that has brought on and protracted the war, speak almost as one as members of this "wise" community of the living dead to whom "this life iss nothing"; it is "merely a room in the inn."[223]

Yet unlike the four Americans (Sartoris, Bland, Monaghan, and the narrator) and the Irishman (Comyn), who have spent three years in their British tunics, the two cultivated and fatalistic sages do not intend, with the fighting's conclusion, to return to the places from whence they came. They have a kind of shelter in the cold kingdom of their thoughts. In the midst of the five angry and drunken pilots they are already residents of their own quiet world where there is talk of music, art, and "victory born of defeat."[224] They envisage a coming order given its flavor by their kind, their brotherhood of ecumenical serenity, free of the excesses of belligerent national feeling. Faulkner uses their agreement on the meaning of things as the centerpiece of this work. And he makes it almost persuasive. Yet finally, in terms of the story's design, it is rejected. Their overt rejection of nationalism produces a riot in a French bar in Amiens, where such advanced views seem out of place to a war-weary, exhausted people. Moreover, their less complicated companions, who defend them against French outrage, cannot join them in the security of stoic rectitude. For this quintet there is only that other brotherhood, with "those who have been four years rotting out yonder" who, says the subadar, "are not more dead than we."[225] In this portion of their teaching he and his

---

222   *Collected Stories*, 407.

223   *Collected Stories*, 426, 420.

224   *Collected Stories*, 413.

225   *Collected Stories*, 421.

equally philosophic friend are confirmed. The difference between what they say and what their solipsistic friends perform is very little indeed. In some dark way, they have all been excluded from life.

Faulkner had a theory about why the first war in the air had so overwhelming an impact on those who fought it: "because there was more concentration [among the pilots] of being frightened ... than in infantry or ground troops." Air combat is a concentration of violence for which no man, however brave, can be prepared. It is a heady taste of power employed, or a dreadful exposure to power applied. And the machines make it terribly impersonal. After a lot of it, with nothing clearly accomplished, men change their habits, their views of life. And they feel close only to those who share their kind of existence, whatever the uniform in which they fly. Finally, they feel trapped by the changes made in themselves by too many patrols. The image the author uses to render this emotion is that of bugs in water, "isolant and aimless and unflagging."[226] He repeats it more than once, suggesting a deterministic frame of reference, invoking the self-pity of an entire generation—the lost generation.[227] The will is easily broken when volition is shown to be an illusion. Again, it is the subadar who sounds the theme, connecting Faulkner once more with the conventional view of his material: "What is your destiny except to be dead? ... It is unfortunate that for the better part of your days you will walk the earth a spirit. But that was your destiny."[228]

Here is a determinism not in evidence in Faulkner's better (and most characteristic) work. We are made uneasy by the emphasis on "the impotence and the need,"[229] the appeal for sentiment not earned by anything shown to us in the text. As he himself came to recognize, when Faulkner wrote most of his World War I fiction he was still too close to the myth of glamorous fatality to shape it to the purposes of his art. There is no irony qualifying the words of Faulkner's narrator. And he says of himself and his old comrades, "[I]n the interval

---

226   *Collected Stories*, 408.

227   *Collected Stories*, 421, 423.

228   *Collected Stories*, 428.

229   *Collected Stories*, 407.

between two surges of the swell we died who had been too young to have ever lived."[230] Only with *A Fable* does Faulkner finally exorcise, get fully in perspective, the romantic phantoms of his youth. There was of course some truth in the view that the static bloodletting of 1915-1918 was a uniquely scarifying ordeal for the young men of the Western World. But history is not, in the rest of the Faulkner canon, an excuse for "giving up," an explanation for total "humility." Not for Henry Sutpen in *Absalom, Absalom!* or Bayard Sartoris in *The Unvanquished* or Chick Mallison in *Intruder in the Dust*. The pride in despair, passivity, and aimless thrashing about tolerated in the war's-end celebrants of "Ad Astra" is of the variety judged harshly in *Go Down, Moses*: judged through the history of Isaac McCaslin and his clan. The enduring, such as appear in the opening section of *Collected Stories*, are not victims of history or of any other external necessity. As we are shown repeatedly—even in many stories composed as early in Faulkner's career as his fiction of World War I—to endure is always in some sense to act. And our awareness of the force of this norm makes a little thin the intended irony of the allusion to a familiar heroic motto in the title of "Ad Astra": *"Per ardua ad astra,[231]"* "with difficulty, to the stars," is expressive of a possibility always present for most of Faulkner's protagonists. It is a measure of what he appears to expect of them—unless they fought in France.

"All the Dead Pilots" is a very weak story. Its only special feature is that it presents the oft-mentioned, almost legendary John Sartoris, aviator and twin brother to Bayard, the central figure in *Flags in the Dust*, Faulkner's first Yoknapatawpha book. Other important characters are a wooden British captain, a guardsman type named Spoomer, a French barmaid called Kitchener (after the British field marshal), "because she had such a mob of soldiers,"[232] and Spoomer's despicable dog. Spoomer and Sartoris are in conflict over the favors of the girl. In consequence of his rank, Spoomer has for a time the advantage in this struggle. Sartoris answers this use

---

230   *Collected Stories*, 408.

231   The motto belongs to the RAF.

232   *Collected Stories*, 514.

of the power to assign duty by manipulating the Englishman's dog and pulling a prank which embarrasses his rival in the eyes of those above them. Spoomer is transferred. Shortly thereafter, Sartoris is killed in combat. It is difficult to find a meaningful pattern in this brief summary. Though its conclusion is somber, the tale itself is low comedy. Furthermore, there is a narrative frame which organizes and contains its unfolding that pulls in still another direction. 1It is through attention to this frame device that we can best understand "All the Dead Pilots" and its relation to the other narratives of World War I.[233] The narrator speaks thirteen years after the time he attempts to reconstruct. Once more we are told of the old pilots that they are now all dead, "dead on the eleventh of November, 1918."[234] What were they like? What set them apart from other men? Are the questions asked and answered [in] this composite account? The narrator is interested in the questions he poses. He probes without sentimentality. It is particularly instructive that he uses Sartoris' quarrel with Spoomer to answer his private inquiry, or rather, Sartoris vs. Spoomer with the report of the former's death attached at the end. This pointless struggle thus concluded "parodies the larger war in which the rivals engaged," and makes of the story a performance of even darker implications than "Ad Astra."

But here frenetic mindless activity replaces talk. The effect of John Sartoris' flaming death, coming after his bizarre encounters with British members of his wing, French soldiers and civilians, and the dog that loved garbage, is that of total irrationality: a bright "flash," a moment's illumination in the darkness, almost degraded by the context in which it appears. Sartoris is not philosophic or glib or broken in spirit. Instead, he is reckless in a way which indicates that, for him, the fighting must be an end in itself. He belongs to nothing. His fortune is an isolation which mocks the military condolence written to this family once he is gone. A poignance is

---

233 Hemingway's *In Our Time* (New York: Boni and Liveright, 1925) uses an over-voice or frame to link the parts of the book into a whole. His connective sections followed a fashion, but were less conventional than Faulkner's. The device is not successfully employed by either author.

234 *Collected Stories*, 511.

added to his death by excerpts from the Mississippi boy's letters home and from his great-aunt's letters to him, and by the story's opening pages concerning old photographs of men who "stood into sight [as] the portent and the threat of what the race could bear and become, in an instant between dark and dark." We are told that images in these snapshots have "a look not exactly human, like that of some dim and threatful apotheosis of the race seen for an instant in the glare of a thunderclap and then forever gone,"[235] which is, despite the uncontested exultation of single combat and the joy of flight, a measure of the melancholy waste of their lives. The narrator cannot find a meaning in these deaths. Not the dignity of a cause. Not even the fellowship of arms. Only "brief glares" in the "wasteland"—Faulkner's title for the section in *Collected Stories* where his accounts of World War I appear.

"Turnabout" is better made than "All the Dead Pilots." It sustains a full action of two parts and is well designed, both for tribute to the craft of the warrior and for correction of the peculiar vanities of tribe and trade. Hemingway liked the story well enough to include it in his anthology *Men at War*.[236] But it too, after a little comic reversal, depends on a surprising and thematically expansive conclusion for its most ambitious effects. And, as in its cognate narrative, the "grim joke" shift of tone does not quite work. This irony, though of a type once in vogue, seems in this case forced and inorganic. Or else it is too abrupt—always a problem with thematically ambitious short stories. We are left with unresolved conflicts. We are urged to throw bricks at the temple, even though we are reminded that neither bricks nor temple exist. But there is more than fashionable cynicism in the last pages of "Turnabout." For the story, even with its arbitrary finale, points forward toward *A Fable* and beyond mere fatalism. The protagonist, Captain Bogard, is in the end neither spiritually dead nor defeated. His anger says to the waste of human grace and

---

235 *Collected Stories,* 512, 511.

236 *Men at War, the Best War Stories of All Time* (New York: Crown Publishers, 1942), ed. Ernest Hemingway.

innocence that something must be changed. In that enterprise he will take a share. But not in the belittling of what his fellow warriors have endured and achieved.

Bogard is an American aviator, a bomber pilot in the American Air Services, but a man of sober and careful habits. He is greatly changed and driven beyond his routine view of war by his encounter with a charming and gallant English midshipman, Claude (L.C.W.) Hope: The American and the young British naval officer meet while both are on liberty in a channel port. Bogard rescues Hope from an entanglement with the military police. The boy is very drunk and is brought by the fliers to their quarters at an airdrome. And then, to be taught what real war is like, he is taken on a bombing raid over German positions. Claude performs well as visiting gunner and enjoys the (luckily) safe landing of Bogard's plane with a bomb hanging half-attached to its right wing. He is modest about himself and interprets Bogard's performance as a display of skill. Also he invites the older American to return his visit and make a patrol at sea. Bogard is terrified by a playful torpedo run in the tiny English craft. Hope and his three shipmates make an especially dangerous run, answering what Hope had seen as Bogard's demonstration for his pleasure. They discharge their torpedo, recover it after a misfire, and then release it again—all of this accomplished under heavy enemy fire, while (or after) dodging mines. The exhausted pilot sends a case of Scotch as a salute to Claude and what he does. Thereafter he reads of the disappearance of Hope's little boat. In anger, he performs an heroic feat during his next flight, imagining as he dives to bomb that his targets are "all the generals, the admirals, the presidents and the kings—theirs, ours—all of them."[237]

On the level of metaphor we are tempted to make something of the midshipman's name. Bogard reacts so forcefully to the death of young Claude because it means a "loss of hope." But this is not quite all that we should say. Hope is youth, innocence, and style. He is completely free of the malaise that infects the talkers in "Ad Astra." He is warm, cheerful, and high-hearted; and he still belongs

---

237 *Collected Stories*, 509.

to home. As in the old poem, he "plays up, and plays the game"—though without vanity or chauvinistic noise. In brief, this boyish sailor is the kind of young man a high civilization cannot afford to waste: like young John Sartoris in courage, but with manners and a gentle spirit. Bogard wants to bomb those indirectly responsible for his death so that no more fine boys will be destroyed by their implicit collusion. Of course, what Bogard's memorial raid explodes is an "ammunition depot" and a "corps headquarters," not a conspiracy to prolong the conflict.[238] To hate what is pointless about the war, to end the fighting swiftly, and then to avoid other conflagrations is the way to recover hope. But not in the spirit of petty national pride, or with the view that modern military power is an instrument of policy. That view has made of all the combatant peoples involved in the Great War culpable agents in the needless sacrifice of their own best blood. Though battle brings out something noble in man, that quality is too precious to be lost when any honorable alternative procedure is at hand, and particularly when war is static, and gets no closer to settling a dispute than peaceful means might be expected to achieve. If peaceful means fail, then only another kind of war is acceptable: one mindful that casualty lists are not mere statistics. Out of this knowledge Bogard continues to fight, and on no other grounds. He feels responsible, joins the company of the enduring, and will never again permit himself the inhumanity of killing as a routine. This is a very hopeful sign, indeed, whatever he may have lost [when he learned of] the sinking of Claude's torpedo boat.[239]

Faulkner's stories of land combat in World War I are as replete with postbellum disenchantment and recollected horror as are his narratives of flight and fliers. But they are, on the whole, more successful than their romantic equivalents. No private myth affects his performance in these works, no special sympathy that might impair the author's judgment or inflate his prose. Two of these fictions are much less derivative of the great body of war literature than are Faulkner's highly stylized tales of air combat. Yet from

---

238   *Collected Stories,* 509.

239   A very popular, often reprinted story, "Turnabout" was produced as a movie by MGM in 1932, with Faulkner writing much of the script.

these earth-bound stories we learn again that men have been greatly changed, disoriented and displaced, by life and death in the blighted fields and trenches of Northern France. There are no exploding flares, no bright moments of illumination followed by hopeless, wistful talk. The process is a slower thing than what we have seen in the stories described above. But if slow, it was nonetheless certain. And once again, its final product was a kind of living death for those who survived its completion—unless they took great care or tried to ignore what they had been about.

"Victory" is a most impressive story. Here form and meaning work together. Its hero, Alec Gray, seems at first glance a victim of history: Europe's, Scotland's, and his own. And certainly, all of these trains and networks of circumstance and inheritance have had a purchase on the young shipwright's life. Europe has called forth its millions from the fixed circle of their private spheres. The Grays are men of duty, firm Lowlanders, who for two hundred years have read the Book, practiced their trade, and "served the Queen in her need."[240] And Alec is an unusually proud and stubborn representative of their kind. But that is finally the trouble. For it is what young Gray does with the given materials of his life that brings him to tragedy in the end.

The blunder of Alec Gray is that he denies his origins, goes against what he is.[241] War has made him an officer, as it had made him a murderer only a short time before—or rather, war and his own inflexible pride, which will not allow him to return to those who love him best, or to the honest and honorable work that he had once known. So, along with so many others lost by changes made in their place or nature during their time in service, Gray declines in penury. He has none of the peacetime contacts which were, before 1914, the normal possessions of the officer class. And he has forgotten the first lesson of the social context from which he came—that there is dignity in any honorable work. He ends up selling matches (begging)

---

240   *Collected Stories,* 442.

241   A fine reading of the story is "Faulkner's 'Victory': The Plain People of Clydebank," by Raleigh W. Smith, Jr., *Mississippi Quarterly,* 23 (Summer 1970), 241-249.

on the street. And, as the story ends, he is furious when one of his old comrades recognizes him in this condition. It is more pathetic that his family has never ceased to await his return or to love him with the fierce possessive love of the Scots for their own.

Faulkner renders with great care the stages by which Alec loses his identity: the place that was his by right of birth. His technique is that of inversion. He begins with Captain Gray at the moment when he most seems the English "milord," during a post-war return to France and the scene of his exaltation. The story's conclusion is the nadir which follows the inevitable collapse of this facade. In between we are told of Gray's origins, the base upon which he had achieved an unusual distinction, and the refuge which that distinction makes him scorn. The entire development is surprising in that Alec, when first in uniform, felt no envy of officers or superiors as a group, nor any desire for promotion or other acknowledgment. Later, he ends up an officer almost by accident because the Grays are brave, so secure in their own rectitude, their hold on a world they helped make, that they require no external reinforcement of their self-esteem. Yet their stubborn assurance, their essential Scottishness, is also a source of conflict. Alec will not accept discipline in what he believes is a private matter. The boy is immature. And he neglects to understand that, as a soldier, he is under a new (and total) regulation. He refuses to shave because he is, by Gray standards, too young. He attracts attention and ends up in military prison. And in retribution for this insult, in an act of private vengeance, he murders the regimental sergeant-major, still ignoring the impersonal nature of war. This leaves his unit without leaders: combat forces him to fill that void. The result is irony. Though it is Gray's merit as a middle-class Lowland Scot that is honored when, after distinguished action, he is trained for an officer, that merit is undermined by his subsequent transformation. Furthermore, it has been compromised from the beginning, though it becomes evident only when he kills his superior. The young shipwright is an officer for too long, becoming just the kind of officer he had hated. And then he is nothing, his place as officer being gone. Throughout these developments the ground base of the senior Gray's warnings sounds as a motif.[242] It is an augury confirmed.

Faulkner, as a Southerner of his generation, could understand how young Scots or Englishmen could be dislocated and displaced through participation in the Great War. As Robert Penn Warren has observed, the impact of this period on his (and Faulkner's) region was far more intense than its impact on the North. It made a social and moral difference not of degree but of kind.[243] The all-absorbing and self-contained pre-modern regime of clan and community, place and prescription, had lost its authority. The results were isolated, disorganized personalities who could find their point of reference only in the battles and camps they had left behind forever—personalities like Captain Gray, whose home is the battlefield where he murdered and put Alec away—or, if not with soldiers, in the hectic life of the nation at war, in motion. After the armistice Gray has achieved no real victory. His role in the enterprise of protecting the empire is at an end. In his post-war excursion in France, he revisits the "scenes of his lost and found life"; but they are "dead" scenes.[244] And he is therefore a quiet specimen of the "living dead." As Faulkner wrote his mother, he had seen Alec Grays on the streets of London during his first visit to that capital in 1925.[245] Certainly, Faulkner could not mistake in such figures one meaning of the recently concluded combat: a meaning on which imagination could feed. For he had come to recognize, even then, that any difficulty comes finally to signify in the life of a man only what he allows it to do to him inside— to his will, his compassion, and his courage. Or, in a larger sense, to his perspective on himself.

---

242   These warnings are all communicated by letters. In the first, his father explicitly condemns his son for "the pride and vainglory of going for an officer. Never mistake your birth, Alec," he writes. "You are not a gentleman. You are a Scottish shipwright" (*Collected Stories*, 447-48). See also pp. 453 and 455. [Ed.]

243   See Warren's "Introduction: Past and Future" in *Faulkner: A Collection of Critical Essays*, ed. Robert Penn Warren (Englewood Cliffs, N.J.: Prentice-Hall, Inc., 1966), 4.

244   *Collected Stories*, 456.

245   *Selected Letters of William Faulkner*, 29. The letter is dated Oct. 7, 1925.

It is essentially instructive to consider Alec Gray in "Victory" in counterpoint to his closest relative in the Faulkner canon, Sgt. Willy MacWyrglinchbeath in "Thrift," the comic story of World War I that was appropriately omitted from the "Wasteland" section of *Collected Stories*. Though this story is apparently derivative of Faulkner's reading and not of his experience, it speaks to the very questions that arise in "Victory" and none of the answers are the same, even though a Scot very like Alec is the person responding. "Wully" differs in being a Highlander, and his background is rural. We do not hear of his family. Furthermore, his fighting is done in the air. Yet he starts the war in the same sort of modest but respectable circumstances that define the Grays of Clydebank. The difference comes from what MacWyrglinchbeath allows his military service to do to his private character. His method of avoiding the living death is assuredly unromantic—he concentrates on saving money. But it is effective. As his commanding officer remarks in approval, "the man who can spend three years in this mess and still look forward to a future with any sanity, strength to his arm, say I."[246] A pilot, Follansbye, uses another formula to describe his Scottish friend: "He was just like a man who, lost for a time in a forest, picks up a fagot here and there against the possibility that he might some day emerge."[247] The Highlander almost ignores the war, except when it comes to doing "his bit." After maneuvering his way into aviation, he flies an observation plane, insures other pilots, and downs a German pursuit craft when his business is interrupted. He wins a decoration, is offered a commission, thanks his superiors for the honor and refuses the rank because it would be expensive. But most of all, he is constantly himself. Though a comic character, a caricature Scot, he never allows violent or dramatic experiences to destroy his judgment or inflate his self-esteem. He preserves his independence and an ordinate pride. And he can even endure with equanimity a small injustice from a neighbor who had kept his stock while he was down in England and over in France. Like the "tall men" in Faulkner's stories of Southern yeomanry, his identity is prior to his activity, an

---

246 *Uncollected Stories of William* Faulkner, ed. Joseph Blotner (New York: Random House, 1979), 390.

247 *Uncollected Stories*, 384.

ontological given not to be shaken by insults or disappointments like the one that moved Alec Gray to kill—and then to become Captain. "Wully" is too one-sided to be a completely normative figure. But he is neither defeated nor dead when the guns go quiet. And if the heroes of Faulkner's other stories of this first modern international war had possessed more of his prudent fortitude, their situations, both in and after the war, would have been far less painful, empty, and desperate than, in most cases, they became. For there is no such thing as a "wasteland" for the thrifty Willy MacWyrglinchbeath.

"Crevasse" is also closely related to "Victory."[248] It was, on first writing, an episode in that longer story, coming after Alec Gray has been commissioned and has returned to the line. But Faulkner wisely concluded that the incident described in this brief episode would appear at its best as an independent fiction and as one of the component parts of the "Wasteland." Indeed, it fits the name given this section of *Collected Stories* better than any of the other fiction gathered with it, while in its small compass it summarizes with a single image what the First World War did to so many young men not prepared to absorb its dehumanizing force.

The extended trope or miniature parable of war that is "Crevasse" is made up of certain unmistakable ingredients. First is the lifeless battlefield, like the far side of the moon except for a few blighted plants.[249] There is a horror about this place. It is a spectral setting, with no birds and no noise—a No-Man's Land, cut off from the outside by a barrage, between the lines. Its propriety as a backdrop

---

248 Raleigh Smith, Jr. comments on the connection of "Crevasse" with "Victory." His criticism is the most useful that we have had, though he may ignore the differences in meaning that result from our not knowing that the Scots captain in the story was originally Alec Gray. If we were to read it as part of "Victory," we would have to focus on Gray's role in the episode. Blotner, in his notes to this tale in *Uncollected Stories* (100-101, 692) suggests that "Crevasse" was removed from "Victory" to tighten the structure of the latter story. Then the narrative was revised to the present tense and all the characters were made anonymous.

249 It is widely acknowledged today that the impression of spiritual devastation conveyed by the WWI battlefield was perhaps most profoundly expressed, in visual terms, by the British painter Paul Nash. See, for example, the painting entitled "The Wire" (1918). [Ed.]

for the living dead is beyond doubt. Of these Faulkner gives us a group of Scots soldiers, including a wounded man and two officers. To complete the figure, there is what these men do in this terrible place. Put in the simplest terms, they attempt to get out, [but] they are not regenerated by this survival. On the contrary, they lose the group identity that had brought them part of the way across the wasteland and emerge from the chalk caves as part of the scene themselves: like the few leaves they have seen, "neither green nor dead."[250] Throughout this journey across and into a man-made hell, the distracted mumblings of the wounded soldier sound as an ironic motif—"A'm no dead! A'm no dead!"[251]

The verbal texture and imagery of "Crevasse" are managed with great skill. The words "death" and "dead" recur. There is a haze, with flashes of fire in the distance. As the soldiers move over the landscape, it grows progressively ominous, barren, and grotesque. Reminders of earlier battles are everywhere. Finally they come to an arena of chalk ridges and strange declivities opening into a mysterious valley of silence where the ordinary distinctions of time do not obtain: "a region, a world where the war had not reached, where nothing had reached, where no life is, and silence itself is dead."[252] When the Scots attempt to cross, the valley floor collapses, dropping them into caves where they confront the grinning remains of gassed Senegalese, buried there years before. Over half of the Scots escape from this entombment, forcing open the sand-covered portals of the cave. They squeeze through a tunnel, toward the light, and, as disparate individuals, perform a parodic celebration of their delivery and rebirth with the wounded man gibbering that he lives, the captain thinking "soon it will be summer," and another soldier "intoning monotonously" from the Bible. Yet the things at which these men rejoice—mere life, the hope of a better day, and the favor of heaven—ring hollow in this case. They have been caught in a trap, a grave. And, once out, they have not really escaped from the fellowship of the skeletal Zouaves, but have instead brought some

---

250   *Uncollected* Stories, 469.

251   *Uncollected Stories*, 471, 472, 474.

252   *Uncollected Stories*, 468.

of the horror of that subterranean place away with them when the fourteen survivors crawl through the narrow opening and crouch on their hands and knees while their wounded comrade (functioning as a chorus) keeps on insisting that they are alive.

As Douglas Day asserts, "Crevasse" is a "superior story."[253] What happens to the Scots soldiers is rendered with great economy. There is no authorial intrusion, no sentimentality, no break in the tone. The result is a minor classic in the literature of war and a narrative interpretation of what happened to an entire generation of young men in the trenches of Northern France. This little allegory reminds us of the darker moments in Stephen Crane. It is one of the more impressive renderings of "the matter of Flanders and Picardy." By it Faulkner has dramatized what the subadar meant in "Ad Astra" when he declared to his celebrating friends that "those who have been four years rotting out yonder … are not more dead than we."

"With Caution and Dispatch" stands as a kind of coda to the full sequence of Faulkner's World War I stories. For though it was first drafted in the early 1930s and is closely related in content to "Ad Astra," to "All the Dead Pilots," and to *Flags in the Dust*, it was not offered for publication until 1940. Like "Thrift," it has a contrapuntal relationship to the more serious components of the series, for it marks an inversion of their treatment of the dream of military glory: an inversion in the direction of the conventional admiring and romantic view of the high adventure of early flying and in the direction of the Sartoris myth. Yet there is no sense of doom or fatality surrounding John Sartoris' high-spirited destruction of three planes while travelling to duty at an airdrome in France. Of this story Hans Skei has rightfully observed that "it does not have much to say about the war itself or the men who fight in it."[254] But it is an interesting evocation of attitudes qualified by the other stories in this set.

---

253   "The War Stories of William Faulkner," 392.

254   Skei, dissertation., 340.

As it appears in these stories, the condemnation of World War I as a waste of life and a nightmare should not surprise those familiar with the rest of Faulkner's work. He distrusted everything men do in a mass. He doubted the ultimate value of machines. And for him, war made complete sense only when waged in self-defense and without paranoia. Furthermore, as Matthew Gray, Alec's father, insists in "Victory," *"When a war gets to where the battles do not even prosper the people who win them, it is time to stop."*[255] Hence we can accept the revulsion of the soldiers in this struggle at the protracted folly of their commanders. We should recall that such is the theme of *A Fable*. Nor is there anything out of the way in the discovery by many of these young warriors that modern military operations leave little room for the grace and excellence of individual valor. Faulkner admired these qualities in the young men who had fought in the War Between the States and earlier American wars. And he was to admire them again in World War II. Posturing, cynicism, and the inference that one bad experience, or bad war, constitutes an indictment of the general frame of things is, thus, a contradiction of most of Faulkner's work. The same may be said of fatalism and self-pity or the idea that traditional values are merely a form of deceit. The mature Faulkner had little patience with what the theologians call the sin of despair. In his view, circumstances do not make the man, except in a few of his early works—including, as we have observed, some stories concerning the "victims" of the First World War.

---

255   *Collected Stories*, 452.

14

A Coda to Sartoris: Faulkner's "My Grandmother Millard and General Nathan Bedford Forrest and the Battle of Harrykin Creek"[256]

The imaginative energy that produced the Sartoris family–in *Sartoris*, "There Was a Queen,"[257] and *The Unvanquished*–was not quite expended in these works. During the years of World War II, in the midst of Faulkner's consciously patriotic phase, he returned once more to "the matter of Sartoris" and made a memorable addition to his chronicle of that worthy family. This addition, "My Grandmother Millard," links the indomitable, gallant Sartoris spirit and the Sartoris' deeds of former days with the American military and political enterprise of the 1940s.

The closest analogue to "My Grandmother Millard" is *The Unvanquished* (1938). The story is almost like an extra chapter of the novel. But not really. For though the central character here, as in *The Unvanquished,* is the corporate spirit of the Sartoris family and the principles of order which it comprehends, particularly in the person

---

256 "A Coda to Sartoris": This essay was originally published in *Critical Essays on Faulkner: The Sartoris Family*, ed. Arthur F. Kinney (Boston: B.K. Hall, 1985), 318-323.

257 "There Was a Queen" is included in *Collected Stories of William Faulkner* (New York: Random House, 1950), 727-744. It was first published in *Scribner's Magazine* in January, 1933.

of its matriarch, Granny Rose Millard, and though the Sartoris clan is brought forward as an epitome of the regime of the Old South, that order in its successful struggle to survive is remembered in this context not as a comment on the South's place in the dialectic of American culture but rather as a prescription or example to strengthen and propel forward the entire nation—the Union it had almost broken—in the great global trial of an international war for survival.[258]

Colonel John Sartoris, in words remembered by the narrator, his son, is the one responsible for objectifying this larger envelope of American history which frames and deepens the story proper, the "courtship" and marriage of Cousin Melisandre (from Memphis) to Lieutenant Philip St.–Just Backus (Backhouse) of Tennessee, with a little special help from General Bedford Forrest and Colonel Sartoris' mother-in-law. Speaking with a high heart, he tells his son Bayard and Bayard's companion, the Negro boy Ringo, "'I won't see it, but you will. You will see it in the next war, and in all the wars Americans will have to fight from then on. There will be men from the South in the forefront of all the battles, even leading some of them, helping those who conquered us defend that same freedom which they believed they had taken from us.'"[259] In other words, that temper which was conquered but not "vanquished" with Appomattox, that "uncomplex will for freedom engaged with a tyrannous machine," could lose battles but "could not be defeated" because "they just willed that freedom strongly and completely enough to sacrifice all else for it."[260]

The freedom of which he speaks is, to be sure, the liberty of a culture or community to be itself, a self-determination of structured "families" of independent people, not a freedom from the social

---

258   Related evidence appears in "Tall Men," "Two Soldiers," and "Shall Not Perish" in *Collected Stories,* 45-61; 61-99; 101-115.

259   *Collected Stories,* 672-673.

260   *Collected Stories,* 672.

bond.[261] Granny plays off the feckless idea of "freedom from" in her remarks to her household after one of the black men on the place begins to talk about what the tide of emancipation will mean once it reaches Yoknapatawpha. During her ritual practice of burying family silver, she declares, "I want all of you free folks to watch what the rest of us that ain't free have to do to keep that way."[262] "Freedom from" here means to be cut off, adrift, beyond the shelter of interdependence. When she invites the restive Lucius to think of himself in that way and points to the road, "he went back to the garden."[263] But defense of the patriarchal (or matriarchal) order is the struggle for the freedom of the possibility of the human community, the association of real persons who are individually fulfilled in their support of each other, and so alive. And even preserving that possibility is worth whatever it costs.

However, though duty and responsibility (the positive names for what Granny calls "not free") are major motifs in "My Grandmother Millard" and though the story ends in a marriage, comedy's traditional image for the promise that civilization will continue, excessive emphasis on these sober concerns exposes us to the danger that will distort the story's flavor and attribute to the author a heaviness of touch not, in this instance, to be proved against him. The tone here is light. No real "dangers" obtrude upon the course of events. Only foolish complications—like Yankees bent upon victory in a war they cannot really win, and the exaggerated delicacy of young Southern girls. Or the foolish notions that some men have—that war is what war is really about. Or if not war, then honor, instead of home and family and the safety of those we love. Rosa Millard's role in correcting these misconceptions is high comedy surrounding

---

261 Liberty in the South meant "the rights and autonomy of communities." See Charles G. Sellers, Jr., ed., *The Southerner as American* (Chapel Hill, 1960), 42; Eugene D. Genovese, *Roll, Jordan Roll: The World the Slaves Made* (New York, 1974), 118-120.

262 "Free" is frequently an ironic term in Faulkner. See, for example, the fourth section of *Go Down, Moses* (New York, 1942), where Isaac McCaslin claims, "Sam Fathers set me free" (300).

263 *Collected Stories*, 669-670.

a moment of low farce. But it suffuses the entire narrative, giving considerable unity to its casual flow. And it is to her performance that we must look in order to read the work.

The story opens with Bayard's account of how his maternal grandmother made all the inhabitants of the Sartoris plantation periodically practice the burying of family silver and other valuables. She is almost a military figure in her timed rehearsals of this operation. Knowing that Memphis has fallen to Federal control and Vicksburg is under siege, she anticipates the arrival of marauding enemy troops. Yet she proposes to allow them to do no more than interrupt the orderly flow of life in her dominion. Part of the labor of preservation is preventing the enemy from changing the way people react and how they can be expected to behave. Another part is restricting the amount of external damage he can do, given the limits of his own moral code. Mrs. Millard is mindful of both of these components of resistance in a fashion that is summarized in the regular burial and unearthing of the precious trunk.[264] Something of what Sartoris[265] means is, of necessity, put by during the turmoil of war. But we can expect it to reappear as soon as the war is done—and even during the war, whenever possible.

For the chatelaine of Sartoris will not completely suspend the order of civility even to protect properties and ways. It is her view that war, even at the worst, must accommodate itself to the central business of life: that the priorities which she represents have precedence over the routines of clash and maneuver and the imperatives of military pride. And for this reason she interrupts the principal Confederate hero for her part of the South and summons him into her parlor from the midst of his campaigns. Asserting her antecedent claims upon his courtesy, she calls him (as Mr. Forrest) from the defense of

---

264   For the importance of this theme in *The Unvanquished* (1938), see my essay, "Faulkner's *The Unvanquished:* The High Costs of Survival," *Southern Review* 14 (Summer 1978), 428-437. I concur with James B. Meriwether that if this story were a part of the novel it would appear as the first episode. See Meriwether, "The Place of *The Unvanquished* in William Faulkner's Yoknapatawpha Series" (Diss., Princeton, 1958, 136, 139).

265   The name "Sartoris" here refers not to a person but to the plantation itself. [Ed.]

northern Mississippi to help her briefly in some important work. As we learn in *The Unvanquished*, Granny finds it difficult to regard the War as anything more than an outburst of interacting male vanities, complicated somewhat by the influence of conflicting ideologies, such as the notions which almost infect Lucius.[266] Therefore, when the conjunction of Melisandre's misadventure in the outhouse and the name of the gallant Confederate officer who rescues her from its destruction produce a verbal and situational irony which obstructs the romance that begins when they first set eyes on one another, the matriarch turns for the instruments of solution to the male authority who is supposed to command the powers she requires.

Bedford Forrest is that figure. He can spell the names of his officers however he wishes. So long as the young lieutenant who has found his "beautiful girl" sitting with the silver chest in the ruins of the Sartoris privy is called Philip St.-Just *Backhouse*, Melisandre can only scream in his presence and flee when he is announced. But the officers and men of General Forrest's command are officially who and what he says they are. And they can be made into whatever he needs them to be—including husbands. Forrest had known "Miss Rosie" in her Memphis years and had been a regular guest in her husband's house. It might be argued that she presumes upon that relation, upon her station and upon his. Yet her ability to ask this much of Forrest, like his response to her message, is a measure of the health and soundness of the regime they both represent.

And he does honor her request, coming in all his dusty grandeur to receive his marching orders. At her bidding (and in keeping with the suggestion of an uncomplicated child, Philip's announced willingness to surrender his name in death), Forrest lists Lieutenant *Backhouse* as officially dead—after first appointing him an honorary brevet major general. Then he "re-creates" the young man as Lieutenant *Backus*.[267] To finish his work at Sartoris, he makes up a

---

266   In *The Unvanquished*, Lucius is less easily corrected; there he is intoxicated by the idea of freedom, betrays Granny, and leaves with the other slaves.

267   The Backhouse genealogy (and original spelling) is not implausible; the name was well known in South Carolina in the eighteenth century, though Backus is, of course, a much more common spelling.

report of the "action" at Harrykin Creek and writes a furlough pass to bring John Sartoris home for the wedding. This metamorphosis is a fragile thing—clearly resting upon the general's emergency powers as military commander of the Confederate States of America in north Mississippi. But it is strong enough to pacify the affected sensibilities of Cousin Melisandre and thus put a check on the troublesome vainglory of the fine boy who is soon to be Cousin Philip as well as arrange for a military wedding which will allow the elders to go about their ordinary business without emotional intimidation from young love.

Granny's trouble was clear to her from the moment when, already recognizing that both boy and girl were incurably "smitten," she hears someone speak Philip's name. The lieutenant's behavior, even when only reported to her, seems to Granny the perfect male equivalent of Melisandre's distraction once he rides away: "she could look at one of them and know all the other Cousin Melisandres and Cousin Philips without having to see them." From past experiences with the species, "she knew more about Cousin Philip than even Ringo could find out by looking at him."[268] But when first invited to take breakfast at Sartoris and consider the problem created by his charge and Granny's charge, Forrest's polite answer includes "why boy."[269]

There has been in his world a brief delay in the unfolding of the consequences from the impasse at Sartoris. But it lasts only until the general attempts to give battle to the Yankees under "Sookey" Smith.[270] At this point the desire of Philip St.–Just Backhouse to lose his name in glorious death proves to be a time bomb that was just

---

268   *Collected Stories,* 679, 680.

269   *Collected Stories,* 689.

270   Despite the date of the dispatches Granny writes for Forrest (28 April 1862), the appearance of General Smith would date the story in February 1863, when Forrest enjoyed his victory at West Point. A second General Smith (A .J.) came against Forrest in June 1864. Faulkner here seems to be relying on folk memories. On Forrest's career, see Andrew Lytle, *Bedford Forrest and His Critter Company* (New York, 1960). [Bradford is correct that of the two General Smiths active in Mississippi during the War, the most likely candidate for the Smith indicated in the text of this story is General William Sooy Smith, ed.]

waiting to explode the well-laid plans of the Wizard of the Saddle. Cousin Philip takes a small force given him to demonstrate in the enemy's front, visits (at dawn) Granny's front yard (and flowerbed) for one more "long, lingering goodbye," and so frightens the Federal forces by his wild charges through their picket that Smith throws out all his cavalry and begins a cautious retreat.[271] Then Forrest knows what boy Mrs. Millard expected him to bring along for breakfast— the most gallant and politically best-connected junior officer in his command, and, so long as he believes his love is hopeless, the most dangerous officer to any plan of entrapping General Smith.

Both Philip and Melisandre are acting out roles in a conventional romantic melodrama: the young officer with his gestures of bravado and exaggerated chivalry, the girl with peculiar mooning patterns for sleep and eating and the composition of wistful poetry and song. And though the girl knows that Backhouse's old and honorable name is not going to keep them apart, she and her love together insist on the importance of certain words that belong to and inform the ritual of fated, hopeless courtly love. Their language on this theme, as in Melisandre's flowery speech to General Forrest and in Cousin Philip's wooden recitation of the Backhouse heritage, remind us of the distance between concept and fact, language and life, as in Lucius's original understanding of "free," Ab Snopes' idea of the "spoils of war," or even the notion of "General" as sometimes entertained by Bedford Forrest. Each, in his own way, is thus brought back to a simpler reality: the truth that the only proper reason for war is to defend civilization, and that the relations between men and women (and of both to children) define what civilizations means— that people, not abstractions, confederate and "cohere."

A sensible woman like Rosa Millard will not be controlled by these "mere counters" because she is a woman intent upon the care and management of real people, existing and living within the orbit of her influence. She represents, as Cleanth Brooks has written, "the

---

271 *Collected Stories*, 692.

nurturing and sustaining force on which a society rests."[272] In her familial vision the being of people is logically prior to their meaning. It is true that portions of the story seem to lack an organic connection to its central thrust—particularly Faulkner's brief glance backward to the account of Granny as a collector of Yankee livestock in *The Unvanquished*. At times the narrative focus appears to wander too far away from Mrs. Millard. And her problems in this imbroglio are no full [measure] of her mettle. She is surrounded by patently comic figures whose "actions...grow out of some image of the self which is carried to the point of affectation."[273] They detract from our sense of her magnificence. And the element of low comedy, linked to a mere verbal irony at the heart of the work, prevents her triumph from being anything half so impressive as the victory of Sartoris in the antecedent novel.[274] Yet it is the same *kind* of triumph. Moreover, the stature of her performance in this upbeat "afterthought" to *The Unvanquished* is not so much diminished by its ease or its context as might at first appear. For Faulkner was correct in the point he was making in most of the fiction that he wrote in the 1940s. To survive in war, a society must preserve its character, its system of values, in private things—even while it engages the enemy without. It must remember why and by whom it was made and not become what it fights against. Granny personifies the determination of her culture to honor the imperatives that Faulkner hopes will be the case with

---

272 Cleanth Brooks, *William Faulkner: The Yoknapatawpha Country* (New Haven, 1963), 99.

273 John Lewis Longley, Jr., *The Tragic Mask: A Study of Faulkner's Heroes* (Chapel Hill, 1963), 113. Longley, whose study is the best previous treatment of this story, appropriately calls it a "comedy of manners," although the low comic elements do not fit this pattern. Melisandre's name may come from the puppet-play in *Don Quixote*, 1, 26, where a puppet-character by that name (spelled Melisendra) is saved by Don Quixote interrupting the puppet show, violently destroying the puppets in the name of chivalry. If this is the source, we have further evidence that this story is not all romantic or high comedy. [Note: It is certainly true that the chivalry of St.-Just Backus has an exaggerated quality that invites comparison with Don Quixote's. The latter imagines that the characters in the puppet show are real people. Both he and Backus live enveloped within a chivalric mist that clouds the distinction between reality and the realm of their dreams, ed.]

274 Meriwether, 136.

the larger American culture of World War II.[275] For these reasons the story ends as it begins—with the Sartoris household practicing the burial and recovery of the silver chest. The exercise, as a trope, is a summary of everything else that occurs as a result of the "battle" at Harrykin Creek.

---

275   See Faulkner to Harold Ober, *Selected Letters of William Faulkner*, ed. Joseph Blotner (New York, 1997), 150.

15.

Text and Context:
Reading Faulkner's *Intruder in the Dust*

The purpose of criticism is to assist readers in reading. When the desire to display ingenuity or bring about social and political change displaces this modest and submissive objective with presently fashionable "heroic" conceptions of the critic's vocation, we may reasonably expect that society will soon put the critic out of business. Literary theory which does not end in the explanation of how books and poems and plays are put together is, in other words, a contradiction in terms. Yet because the form of any work of art is rooted in its place and time as it aspires to reach beyond them, because that focus is always incommensurate with its discursive explanation, criticism is always a difficult, incomplete process. What I mean by this predication I will attempt to illustrate in discussing one of William Faulkner's most puzzling and neglected works, a novel concerning race written before the Second Reconstruction[276]— before anyone knew that it would occur.

---

276   While the term "Second Reconstruction" usually refers to the Civil Rights era, which focused especially on bringing segregation to an end, it is possible that Bradford here was thinking of an *ongoing* second Reconstruction, one that today, in its fanatical destruction of southern monuments, seems intent on the complete erasure of southern history. Though Dr. Bradford's death preceded most of the iconoclasm we have witnessed in more recent years, attacks on display of the Confederate battle flag were already well underway during his lifetime. [Ed.]

The place of *Intruder in the Dust* in the canon of Faulkner's fiction is a question not easy to resolve.[277] Though a very successful novel, widely read, and the source of a successful film, the book eludes description. It is not often taught by Faulkner scholars and has been ignored or dismissed as unimportant by critics representing almost every imaginable approach to serious fiction. Nonetheless, it marks a central moment in Faulkner's career as he comes, after the *Unvanquished* and *Go Down, Moses,* to step even further away from the tradition of literary modernism, toward an even stronger commitment to the narrative of "knightly" adventure tales of the unfolding character of the gentleman as a figure necessary to social cohesion, justice, and peace in any regime imaginable. The Faulkner of *Intruder in the Dust* is the Faulkner of the Nobel Prize speech (1950) and of the masterpiece of his old age, *The Reivers* (1962). It is not an anomaly among his works but is, nonetheless, fiction which presents certain difficulties to the contemporary reader. I will attempt to detail a few of these and to suggest a way around them to assist readers in deciding for themselves what they think about the book.

Intruder in the Dust is a novel in three parts. Its protagonist is a sixteen-year-old Mississippi boy, Charles "Chick" Mallison, nephew of Gavin Stevens, lawyer and sometimes county attorney in Yoknapatawpha County. Chick is the intruder in Faulkner's title because he (with a black friend of his own age, Aleck Sander, and an elderly white gentlewoman, Miss Habersham) goes out to Caledonia Chapel in Beat Four, the most remote and most violent part of Yoknapatawpha, and opens the grave of a recently murdered member of the Gowrie family, the most violent residents of that all-white enclave. What the Mallison boy finds inside of what is supposed to

---

277 The standard treatments of *Intruder in the Dust* (New York: Random House, 1948) are: Andrew Lytle, "Regeneration for the Man," *Sewanee Review*, 57 (Winter 1949), 120-127; Cleanth Brooks, *William Faulkner: The Yoknapatawpha Country* (New Haven: Yale University Press, 1963), 279-294 and 420-424; and Michael Millgate, *The Achievement of William Faulkner* (New York: Random House, 1966), 215-220. There is also some instruction in William Gold, *William Faulkner: A Study in Humanism, From Metaphor to Discourse* (Norman: University of Oklahoma Press, 1966), 76-93.

be Vinson Gowrie's grave immediately alleviates the problems which sent him into that territory, for the consensus of opinion in the town of Jefferson before Chick (with his two cohorts) takes action is that the murder has been (it seems) committed by Chick's unusual friend, Lucas Beauchamp, an elderly mulatto who is a proud relative of the white McCaslin family, one of the oldest in that part of Mississippi. There is circumstantial evidence implicating Lucas. But the old man has had an earlier experience with Chick which persuades him that the boy will help to exonerate and preserve him from the probability of being lynched. He is correct in his presumption.

The first of the three sections in this novel runs through the first three chapters,[278] including when Lucas loses patience with lawyer Stevens and asks Chick to go out to Caledonia, dig up Vinson Gowrie, and look at him—because Lucas has a forty-one Colt revolver and Gowrie wasn't shot by such an antique gun. Lucas and Chick are connected by what happened when, four years earlier, Chick had fallen into a creek on the old man's place. Out of that *contretemps* grew a real, though unlikely, relationship between the two as persons, a contest in courtesy between them made necessary by Chick's original, unthinking insult to Lucas in Lucas' cabin.[279]

Chapters four through eight[280] make up the second movement in this novel and include the fragment of a mystery story for which Faulkner had accepted a Random House contract in 1940. This part of the novel (apart from a few passages added just before the work was finished) has a tone which does not seem appropriate in so serious a book. There is instead a spirit of cheerful inquiry into a problem about a death that requires a solution, but no concern with the danger faced by the three unlikely detectives. The focus is on the process of ratiocination, not on justice for Lucas Beauchamp or protection for the misguided people of Yoknapatawpha, those who make up what Chick calls "the face."

---

278 *Intruder*, 1-73.

279 The "insult" to which Bradford refers here is probably Chick's attempt to offer Lucas money after he saved Chick from drowning in a pond near Lucas's cabin. [Ed.]

280 *Intruder.*, 74-179.

Then, in section 3 of the novel, the pacification of Chick's troubled spirit,[281] of his shame and outrage at his neighbors' prejudgment of an innocent man and their hushed expectation of a corporate crime, follows the external resolution of the novel. Crawford Gowrie is identified as the killer of his brother, and of Jake Montgomery too, a timber buyer with whom Crawford has been in business. The mob in Jefferson who have waited for the lynching of Lucas are dispersed in embarrassment. Old Mr. Nub Gowrie (who is the moral superior of all the would-be witnesses to a lynching) helps to bring into jail his murderous son. Only at that point may Chick and his uncle Gavin argue out the meaning of these events, probing one another in a series of exchanges about the enveloping action of the novel [and] the meaning of Southern history. Chick's continuing identity with the place of his birth is at stake in their conversations and in how he receives Gavin's now-infamous speeches about preserving the moral and political independence of the South.[282] At one level, the book *is* a parable about the relation of the sections within the context of the United States and about the worthlessness of racial reforms that are merely "given" to the Negro before he has earned them. These teachings are validated by the plot of *Intruder in the Dust* and not by their relation to some extrinsic paradigm. At the end of the book, Gavin and Chick think as one about their "obligations." They think as Faulkner thought until his death in 1962, a fact we can easily determine from his letter to Paul Pollard, his onetime servant, who asked Faulkner to subscribe for him a lifetime membership in the NAACP.[283] Yet the book is also about the sources and reserves within the Southern tradition that should bring to Lucas and to other capable members of his race the justice that their merit deserves, and then to the rank and file of American blacks the kind of dignity that will (without threatening white civilization) foster a lasting *entente* between the races. As Gavin tells Chick, "Don't quit."

---

281   *Intruder,* 180-247.

282   *Intruder,* 153-156; 194-196; 203-206; 215-217.

283   The original manuscript of the letter in question, dated Feb. 24, 1960, is held in the University of Virginia archives. It is also included in *Selected Letters of Williams Faulkner,* ed. Joseph Blotner (London: The Scolar Press, 1977), 443-44. [Ed.]

The book is not concluded until Lucas and Gavin have settled their business in a context of comic formality and we have seen Lucas walk the streets of Jefferson seemingly ignored by the hosts of people around him, yet made forever special by his moral advantage over them. Then Lucas is obliged to make his manners to Miss Habersham for having regarded him as family, since his late wife, Mollie, had been a Habersham Negro. But Chick's moment of resolution had come earlier, when he had walked all alone around the empty square of Jefferson, "...unhurried and solitary but nothing at all of forlorn, instead with a sense a feeling not possessive but proprietary, viceregal, with humility still...."[284]

The evidence of structure in reading Faulkner's *Intruder in the Dust* is, for the critic, always the most important evidence, even in this heyday of deconstruction and the new literary history, for structural evidence is stubborn and recalcitrant in its resistance to manipulation. That plot, which details an instance of knight errantry, of chivalric journey out and back, has one set of implications, even if turned upside down by irony. It has a meaning which cannot be "seized" through the instruments of willful subjectivism. Like the youthful Isaac McCaslin (*Go Down, Moses*) and Bayard Sartoris (*The Unvanquished*) and Lucius Priest (*The Reivers*), Chick is an apprentice in the ancient tradition which stands behind the figure of the gentleman. It maintains, among other things, that some men will always be more responsible than others, will feel a sense of obligation to act in *loco parentis*. With the linguistic surface of the novel it is possible to play ingenious games. But the fable of the book is another matter.

The biggest problem that the modern reader has with *Intruder in the Dust* is his disposition to make of Lucas Beauchamp its only important character. Subsidiary and related predictabilities are that the contemporary [reader] will so dislike Gavin's speeches that he cannot see their relationship to the education of Charles Mallison. All of this comes from our inclination to see coercive racial reform as one of the few still sacred causes, and to find in

---

284   *Intruder*, 211.

victims the best arguments for it. Much of the decorum of *Intruder in the Dust* and of its realistic image of Mississippi life in the 1940s is lost in the process, for William Faulkner did not think that way. Another difficulty that moderns have with Faulkner's most political novel is that they misunderstand the idea of community affirmed by Chick and Gavin when they insist that Negroes should, by stages, be permitted to become all that they can become. Many readers are still bothered by the cheerful tone of detective fiction in those middle chapters. And finally, the thread of Southern nationalism or particularism still alive in Faulkner when he wrote *Intruder in the Dust* is now unrecognizable and inexplicable to most young Americans—even to young Southerners. But that particularism is at the very heart of the book:

> For every Southern boy fourteen years old, not once but whenever he wants it, there is the instant when it's still not yet two o'clock on that July afternoon in 1863, the brigades are in position behind the rail fence, the guns are laid and ready in the woods and the furled flags are already loosened to break out and Pickett himself with his long oiled ringlets and his hat in one hand probably and his sword in the other looking up the hill waiting for Longstreet to give the word and it's all in the balance, it hasn't happened yet, it hasn't even begun yet, it not only hasn't begun yet but there is still time for it not to begin against that position and those circumstances which made more men than Garnett and Kemper and Armstead and Wilcox look grave yet it's going to begin, we all know that, we have come too far with too much at stake and that moment doesn't need even a fourteen-year-old boy to think *This time. Maybe this time* with all this much to lose and all this much to gain: Pennsylvania, Maryland,

the world, the golden dome of Washington itself to crown with desperate and unbelievable victory the desperate gamble, the cast made two years ago....[285]

In the medieval sense of the term (as Dante employs it in his *Divine Comedy*), *Intruder in the Dust* is high comedy. All the elements of Yoknapatawpha are rejoined, reconnected at the novel's end. But not before Jefferson has been reminded of its shortcoming—and of its oldest and most honorable traditions. The book turns on a plausible accident—that Lucas, a restless widower, is out walking when some timber is stolen and when Vinson Gowrie is killed—there with his antique pistol, a gun he has recently fired at a rabbit. But none of this is possible without Lucas' astonishing independence, his responsibility for himself, his courage, and his identification with his white ancestors (though he is not ashamed of their black counterparts). When cursed by a white man he meets at a country store, and defined as part of the Edmonds' establishment, he responds, "I ain't a Edmonds. I don't belong to these new folks. I belongs to the old lot. I'm a McCaslin." With his fine hat, black broadcloth suit, heavy watchchain and gold toothpick, he is a figure out of the southern past—a man of tradition even in his stubbornness, and his vices. Drawing on the resources of that past, treating Chick as one gentleman does another, he instructs him in the fact that all blacks are not the same—and that their future as part of the South will depend on how much they come to resemble Lucas, who has his great reserve of dignity within—and will not be dependent on how unknowing whites receive him. Even Lucas' reluctance to do much in his own defense is part of his peculiar station in his section of Mississippi. One cannot imagine him joining a group to practice civil disobedience, though he is more trouble to those who ignore or deny his worth, a bigger cause of shame, than any group could be.

It was by way of thinking on Lucas and on other blacks of equivalent worth and merit that Faulkner brought himself to recognize the weakness of Jim Crow as a system of postbellum social

---

285 *Intruder*, 194-195. The words in this passage are an expression of Chick's thoughts. [Ed.]

control and "confederation." That is precisely how most Southern conservatives—even before 1954—came to worry about that set of institutions borrowed, in all of its rigidity, from the North by their/our ancestors after the War between the States.[286] Civilized and responsible blacks could not forever be legally disadvantaged merely for reasons of color without creating uneasiness among white Southerners like Gavin and Chick, for that arrangement, if inflexible applied, dehumanizes both its perpetrator and its subject—resulting (for the former) in shame or savagery. Hence, Chick's anger at "the face" of Jefferson's corporate determination to make Lucas "just a nigger"—the mistake he himself had made earlier as a guest in Lucas' home. Formally speaking, Lucas is important in *Intruder in the Dust* for what he does to Chick. Just as Gavin is important for the same reason. And Miss Habersham. And Aleck Sander. And even Old Man Gowrie, as he holds the body of his son and wipes wet sand from his eyes.

Finally, a word about Gavin's long speeches. They are a dramatic necessity in *Intruder in the Dust*. (And they are not all Gavin's.) This is in no way to argue that they (or Chick's anger with Jefferson which draws them out of Stevens) are simplistic reflections of the author's own 1948 opinions. For one thing, Gavin is much more the optimist than William Faulkner, and a public man all of his life, while the writer (even in his vatic phase) only occasionally accepted that role. Also, Faulkner is only sometimes florid, while Gavin is persistently given to the "high style." But from the thrust of the novel as a whole it is clear that [Gavin's lengthy utterances] are not primarily ironic. In the book's conclusion these speeches, as a series, reach a point where they become organic components of a sequence, a structured whole. They are realized functionally in the uncle/nephew relationship which Chick and Gavin achieve: a relationship which, because of the circumstances provoking their loquacity, includes certain presumptions in political theory. In order to prevent Chick from

---

286　See Leon Litwack, *North of Slavery: The Negro in the Free States, 1790-1860* (University of Chicago Press, 1961). That Jim Crow laws were, ironically, first encoded in Massachusetts, and from there spread to other northern states and communities, is by now well established, if often ignored in the popular media. [Ed.]

drifting away into alienation and exile from the culture that produced him, he must be reminded of Appomattox and Reconstruction, of how the Negro came to be, not a confederated part of the Southern *gemeinschaft*, but the "enemy-within," the fifth column within the Southern order which Yankees were accustomed to using any time they wished to enact their favorite moral melodrama, or any time they had designs on the political integrity of the buried nation "down there"—below the Old Surveyors' Line.

In this purpose we know Gavin is successful since Chick tells us, before he walks the square alone in the "proprietary" passage quoted above, that he is now prepared to make, with respect to his own people, "that furious almost instinctive leap and spring to defend them from anyone anywhere." The passage is expressive of tribal politics by which Americans not Southern are often puzzled. Then Chick comes in the end to contain and render his dialogue with Gavin within himself.[287] His concern with the "homogeneity" of all of Southern society, his commitment to the regime, to cultural oneness, emerges directly from this painful process of education by both events and speech. Though if we anachronize such evidence, it can only confuse, becoming finally a reason for overemphasizing some aspects of our recognition of the book as a finished (if imperfect) whole.

Our problems with *Intruder in the Dust*, then, should encourage us to recognize that Faulkner's fiction cannot be read in a vacuum. The Mississippi of the nineteenth and early twentieth centuries is the raw material of most of his work. Without what Aristotle calls the "accidents" of Southern life, as he knew it, he could make no fiction. And it is through our attention to the concreteness and particularity of his rendering, through our recognition of the voice speaking to us, that we come to understand the universal themes which he explores and the depth of his engagement with them. If we are too put off by his raw material, his "lumber," and his persona as Southern sage and bard, then we will never get to the point of reading him and knowing whether or not we like his work. Moreover, if we ignore the evidence

---

287   *Intruder*, 211-217.

of structure as a key to other elements of his craftsmanship, we are likely to imagine that we can read him insofar as we have subjected him to the concerns and assumptions of our own time. Such new literary history records nothing but arrogance, presumption, and bad aesthetics.

16.

The Great Enterprise[288]

Faulkner studies stand as a miniature and summary of all that is fashionable in modern literary criticism, and it also presents a window on what has gone wrong with the great enterprise of reading and absorbing the texts which, with an attendant body of commentary, lie at the heart of our intellectual tradition. More than with any other modern writer, the literary community has, in the past forty years, attempted to interpret William Faulkner—has discussed him so industriously and from so many perspectives that Faulkner studies are now at the center of its vocation and a measure of its success. This undertaking continues to mirror both the accomplishments and the shortcomings of all contemporary literary scholarship—even though no one can be expected to keep up a thorough account of its rapid accumulation or its multifaceted eccentricity.

Despite there being, even now, more Faulkner scholarship than makes any sense, we must admit that within this unabating flood appear from time-to-time new works that are either useful or symptomatic—that play some distinctive role in the still unfinished business of understanding Faulkner. To my surprise one of these con-

---

288 This essay was first published in *The Sewanee Review*, Vol. 100, No. 4 (Fall 1992), 700-705.

tributions is Susan Snell's *Phil Stone of Oxford: A Vicarious Life*.[289] The importance of the biography is unexpected because of the attitude toward Phil Stone that Professor Snell describes, a view of the man widely accepted for these last thirty years, whose proponents have been unjustly inclined to undervalue his contribution as Faulkner's mentor and muse.[290]

To understand that undervaluation and its causes is not difficult. Stone's frequent bitterness toward Faulkner as the novelist moved from triumph to triumph while the Yale-educated lawyer spiraled downward toward ruin offended most of the younger scholars and journalists who came to him for information about Faulkner's beginnings—his origins and apprenticeship. The less Faulkner acknowledged the large role of the literary attorney in his "education," the more influence Stone claimed. Denigration of Stone became a convention. Yet, though Faulkner was, in his last decade, often filled with outrage at what Stone said, did, and reported about him, the relationship between the two men was too close and too much an essential part of their lives ever to be shattered. This is not to say that Philip Avery Stone ever completely understood William Cuthbert Faulkner or his work. But Stone's family stories, his own adventures, and his experiences *with* William Faulkner were an integral part of the younger man's fiction. And this leaves aside Faulkner's creative use and study of Phil Stone himself in the figure of Gavin Stevens and in his accounts of other well-bred but indecisive Southerners of good family, often incapable inheritors of the active and competent tradition of the gentleman that they intend to affirm.

There are, to be sure, difficulties with any kind of biographical criticism. An author's domestic relations, his politics, and even his taste in food do not run in a straight line into explanations of his handiwork. And the connection of life and art is even more remote

---

289   Susan Snell, *Phil Stone of Oxford: A Vicarious Life* (Athens: University of Georgia Press, 1991).

290   Faulkner's relationship with Phil Stone, a Yale-educated lawyer and classicist in Oxford, began in 1914 when Stone was 21 and Faulkner 17. At least in those early years, Stone's influence on his younger protégé's reading and writing was crucial to his intellectual and literary development. [Ed.]

when we are talking about the biography—the habits, attitudes, and financial circumstances—of a writer's close friend. Furthermore, Professor Snell gives us too much psychological explanation of her subject and too much gratuitous observation on the shortcomings of male Southerners of a conservative disposition. In this vein she offers us nothing more than political correctness. Yet, all such justifiable complaints aside (some of them owing to the influence of Mrs. Emily Stone), this book will have a permanent place in the study of Faulkner's achievement. It has been thoroughly done and will interest all serious students of Faulkner's fiction—successful as a narrative and full of amazing stories, not all of them utilized as raw material by the reshaping power of Stone's gifted friend, the one called "the poet" by their friends in the Clarksville and Memphis demimonde. These would give the book value, even if it had no other purpose.

Unlike Snell's *Phil Stone of* Oxford, Frederick Karl's *William Faulkner: American Writer*[291] has no redeeming qualities to make up for its author's addiction to anachronism, psychological speculation, and the affirmation of his own conventional political attitudes. I agree with Karl's distinction between Faulkner's fondness for modern techniques in rendering consciousness and his doubts about "the values of that encroaching modernism." He understands his subject as a man who "profoundly feared change." Yet he at times imagines Faulkner as a mere progressive, a figure who is nowhere visible in the details of the novelist's life. Moreover, Karl postures endlessly, pushing trendy platitudes or huffing along page after page in uneasy reaction when Faulkner uses a racial epithet without intending anything pejorative by his choice of words. Or Karl does something even worse when he finds implications in Faulkner's text that are inconsistent with his reading of the man's character. All of this affected outrage and virtue may serve Mr. Karl's sense of his own moral worth—or to assert his merits among his readers. But, along with his efforts at psychobiography, they ruin his reading of Faulkner—even though he is sometimes useful or instinctive on specific books or stories.

---

291   Frederick R. Karl, *William Faulkner: American Writer* (Weidenfeld & Nicolson, 1989).

Some obvious (though partial) explanations account for Faulkner's imaginative achievement—explanations proceeding from the relationship of his art to history and biography. Probabilities in the life of a man of his class and generation play out in what he writes. And we can say this much without farfetched psychological conjecture or political gymnastics in search of ideological overtones. *Thinking of Home: William Faulkner's Letters to His Mother and Father, 1918-1925*[292] is a gathering of Faulkner's reassuring and cheerful letters to his parents—letters from New Haven, Toronto, New York, New Orleans, and Europe. They tell us unequivocally that though young William's journey and his closely related choice of vocation made no sense to his father, Murray, his mother, Maud, gave strong support to his aspiration as an artist. Even Professor Karl can write that "Maud's belief in [her son] was complete and unbreakable." And an aspect of this support was her confidence in his future as an artist. In his life, both practical and creative, she was "a long shadow, both presence and influence." As authority figure she validated her son's decision to reject the normal southern patterns for male self-fulfillment and released him to explore the realms of sensibility.

Though in these letters he considers his audience and affirms a special secret about his plans that he shares with his mother, Faulkner also reveals much of what was on his mind during his apprenticeship and how these long journeys far from home figure in the plan of his career. They were part of an experience of the world which he believed an author's life required. On October 17, 1925, he wrote his father that "I have been away from our blue hills and sage fields and things long enough"—indicating an accomplished objective, which for Murry he connected with much seeing. From New Orleans and Paris the young Faulkner draws a detailed and optimistic account of the externals of literary life. He speaks enthusiastically about writers he has come to know. Moreover, he sometimes "practices" on his

---

292 *Thinking of Home: William Faulkner's Letters to His Mother and Father, 1918-1925,* ed., James G. Watson (Norton, 1991).

parents, filling out and rendering as action the account of this or that small adventure, describing scenes, people and episodes just as they were about to appear in *Sartoris* or *Soldier's Pay.*

These epistolary demonstrations of craft are inventions and not "true." But they are part of his attempt to establish, for his parents, who he is—what Phil Stone thinks he is going to be and his literary friends in New Orleans think he is becoming. These letters (from a collection preserved at the University of Texas at Austin) are not so good as those collected by Joseph Blotner in his *Selected Letters of William Faulkner*,[293] but nonetheless they are of value in one's tracing of Faulkner back to his beginnings, his first imagining of himself as man and author—in Watson's phrase "writing himself into being."

This "family" correspondence shows William Faulkner as a social being, one who cannot fully exist outside a circle of people, who is never cut off from home even when he is far away. As the years passed, none of this situation changed very much, even after his father died. Indeed, for a time, this Mississippi rootedness preserved him from all the demons which [might have driven] him away from what is central in human experience into a vainglorious and destructive isolation. The collection of these 140 letters, two postcards, and two telegrams constitutes a major contribution to Faulkner scholarship. Watson's introduction to the edition is excellent, reminding us as it does that Faulkner had a largely happy childhood, and that he enjoyed much support in getting started as a writer.

Study and interpretation of Faulkner's early letters is assuredly valuable work. Most recent Faulkner criticism does too little to help us read the fiction with which it is ostensibly concerned, being instead occupied with certain political or theoretical questions. Yet there is a new book, *Faulkner's Short Fiction*,[294] by James Ferguson of Hanover College that propels the "Faulkner industry" forward as do few other contributions to the field: It helps to remedy an

---

293 *Selected Letters of William Faulkner*, ed. Joseph Blotner (New York: Random House, 1977).

294 James Ferguson, *Faulkner's Short Fiction* (University of Tennessee Press, 1991).

oversight in the scope of this research, a relative silence about that part of Faulkner's narrative achievement around which he organized the practical details of his life. During a period of [roughly] twenty years (1930 – 1950) Faulkner made much of his living writing short fiction, producing in the end almost one hundred narratives that were shorter than full-length novels, plus familiar essays, sketches, reviews, and reminiscence. I have complained of this critical neglect of the short fiction for more than thirty years. But that neglect has begun to change in recent years as a number of studies, in addition to Ferguson's have been published: Anthony P. Libby's *Chronicles of Children: William Faulkner's Short Fiction* (1976); Philip Momberger's *A Critical Study of Faulkner's Early Sketches and Collected Stories* (1976); and James B. Carothers' *William Faulkner's Short Stories* (1985). Hans Skei's groundbreaking *William Faulkner: The Novelist as Short Story Writer: A Study of William Faulkner's Short Fiction* (1985) organized and provided an overview of the entire subject. More recently, we have a new volume of essays with the same focus, *Faulkner and the Short Story* (1992).

But Ferguson's book is the most ambitious and successful critical discussion of Faulkner's short stories to appear thus far. *Faulkner's Short Fiction* is a judgment of its subject and not a survey. It is inclusive, for the author considers nearly all the stories and all the ways in which they are related to other Faulkner fiction and to one another. Only here and there is it touched by the anachronism that corrupts most Faulkner scholarship.

Ferguson is very persuasive on the shortcomings of Faulkner's weaker stories, good on the form of the stories, the thematic patterns for grouping them under particular headings, on kinds of narrative technique displayed in their canon and on how they have been organized in several collections. He argues as much for the unity of these collections as can be maintained. No elaborate theory on these harmonies can be very impressive, however, since the stories were written first and only then assembled. According to this acute critic Faulkner's best short stories include such obvious classics as "Red Leaves," "That Evening Sun," "A Rose for Emily," "Dry September," and "Barn Burning," as well as neglected works such as "A Courtship,"

"Tomorrow," "Mountain Victory," and "A Justice." And a good (though mixed) case can be made for another ten or twelve such as "Lo!," "There Was a Queen," and "Race at Morning"—stories that Ferguson does not admire. His conception of the art of short fiction is totally modernist and most demanding—excluding stories that are told in the broad and partially sententious traditions of rural tale, of the parable and of heroic narratives which have purposes different from Faulkner's modernist masterpieces. But the conclusion to this book is one that moves us to belief: "When we consider the total body of Faulkner's short fiction, we must conclude that, like his novels, it reveals an astonishing scope and variety, a fertility, energy and inventiveness unmatched by any other American writer.

On the roots of Faulkner's fiction in his region's folk culture and in its early literary history Daniel Hoffman speaks eloquently in his *Faulkner's Country Matters: Folklore and Fable in Yoknapatawpha,*[295] Hoffman knows what Ferguson sometimes overlooks—that one part of Faulkner belongs not to the indirect and ironic phase in the history of the Republic of Letters but to the oral tradition and Mississippi, to memory and the old task of the poet to refine and transmit his particular culture in rehearsing its myths. Hoffman is very helpful on those Faulkner novels which, in some respects, appear to be collections of independent narratives. In responding to deconstructionist, post-Marxist, and structuralist readings of "The Bear" he is generally successful. And, in answering readings of Faulkner infected by an ahistorical cosmopolitanism, he is close to giving definite correction. A writer's subject has a referent outside the imagination's feverish context through which that material is transformed. Aristotle was correct: our primary concern in interpretation should be devoted to plot or "action." And the solipsism of contemporary conceptions of poetic creation are not the equivalent of what occurs in the process of making, the process that the poet experiences. In writing "contextual and formal analysis," Hoffman (according to his own description) "does not proceed from

---

295   Daniel Hoffman, *Faulkner's Country Matters: Fable and Folklore in Yoknapa-tawpha* (Baton Rouge: Louisiana State University Press, 1989).

a contemporary sense of grievance [or a] perceived injustice in the treatment of race or sex, to be assuaged at the expense of the integrity of fiction." Hence we should take his work seriously.

Unfortunately, what I say of the Ferguson and Hoffman books I can maintain of only a few other recent additions to the vast corpus of Faulkner criticism. Ideas concerning the present political value of literature overwhelm almost every other consideration in most of the trendy nonsense—ideas which outweigh even that of aesthetic delight, clearly of importance only to a "decadent ruling class." An instance of this ideologically "correct" criticism (always the bane of Faulkner scholarship, even before the flourishing of critical theory) is John N. Duvall's *Faulkner's Marginal Couple: Invisible, Outlaw and Unspeakable Communities.*[296] According to Professor Duvall his reasons for reading Faulkner (which have been almost overcome by the onset of political correctness) include a desire "to lend whatever small support I, as a man, might to improving the conditions of women in our society." His is a political preoccupation of such directness as to leave us all but speechless. Until he was able to write about Faulkner and thereby support the cause of "liberal feminism," it was his fear that he might have to give up his subject altogether. Duvall tells us that he has found in the South many "colleagues who would not teach Faulkner because they felt uneasy with his fictional world." His device for resolving this dilemma is in discovering scattered in Faulkner's texts "deviant couples" who are there not to assert the norm indirectly but to challenge it. It would be, we must conclude, all for the best if Mr. Duvall followed the example of his friends, gave Faulkner back to the "old order" and found another author to champion his advanced views. For, as we learn from *Faulkner's Marginal Couple,* in the other way lies chaos and dark night, both for the cause of women and that of honest critical exposition.

---

296   John N. Duvall, *Faulkner's Marginal Couple: Invisible, Outlaw and Unspeakable Communities* (Austin: University of Texas, 1990).

But we must not expect well of Faulkner studies, so long as there is so much of it, and so many reasons for its manufacture. For a time, though, we can be sure that such studies will continue to get (with certain volumes excepted) in the way of reading Faulkner.

www.ingramcontent.com/pod-product-compliance
Lightning Source LLC
Chambersburg PA
CBHW061524020726
47502CB00006B/2219